Quentin Corn

OTHER YEARLING BOOKS YOU WILL ENJOY:

YEARLING BOOKS/YOUNG YEARLINGS/YEARLING CLASSICS are designed especially to entertain and enlighten young people. Charles F. Reasoner, Professor Emeritus of Children's Literature and Reading, New York University, is consultant to this series.

For a complete listing of all Yearling titles, write to Dell Readers Service, P.O. Box 1045, South Holland, Illinois 60473.

MARY STOLZ

Quentin Corn

ILLUSTRATED BY PAMELA JOHNSON

A YEARLING BOOK

Published by
Dell Publishing Co.
a division of
The Bantam Doubleday Dell Publishing Group, Inc.
1 Dag Hammarskjold Plaza
New York, New York 10017

For all my dear family, who have
been so kind to Quentin Corn, and
to Q's friend and ours, Noel Perrin
—M.S.

Quentin Corn

CHAPTER ONE

The sun rose and shone upon the pig's dwelling. It shone on the muddy wallow and on the mucky yard, on the wooden trough and the water bucket. Its light entered the pig's house and he awoke.

For a while he did not move. He lay where he was, on clean and shining straw, gazing out. What he saw was what he always saw. The wallow, the yard, the trough, and the wall going around it all. He was looking at the space where he was penned, which was what he mostly looked at, morning, noon, night.

He got up, trudged into the yard, put his front feet on the trough, and looked over the wall at the farm. That was the other view he now and then tormented himself with. There there was no wall keeping creatures penned. There was the farmhouse, the big barn, the fields beyond.

He watched the other animals. The horse, Quentin. A dog, Sam. A lot of cows and some cats. All of them going about perfectly free. Even the *chickens* were at liberty.

And here he was, walled, alone, lonely.

"This pig life," he said to himself, "is the perfect bottom of the barrel, and I am finished with it."

If not a pig, though, what to be? A cow, lolling in the meadow with other cows to keep him company? Rather a pleasant life, but possibly a dull one. He had better not rush into anything. The idea was to think carefully and decide which animal really had the best of it.

Not a chicken. The turnover among the chickens was awful to consider. And though he did not wish to be unkind (he was a warmhearted pig), chickens were just about brainless. Probably not their fault, as they had such little heads, but no pig would choose to become a chicken when he chose not to remain a pig.

All the world recognized that pigs were brainy.

On that basis, he mused, the horse was eliminated too. Quentin was as handsome a creature—next to a pig— as anyone could wish to see, but he submitted to being saddled, or harnessed to a cart or—in winter—to a sugar sled. He worked too hard, which was not smart at all. So he was not as free as he looked.

The dog was bright. But this pig had never fancied dogs. Too much tail-wagging and isn't-our-master-marvelous about them. Cats, now. There was an animal *nobody* bossed around. But he didn't think he had the personality —mysterious and silent—to be a successful cat.

At this point in his reflections, the pig looked up to see the farmer, the master, his *owner*, Mr. Quigley, coming toward him to dump some mashed potatoes and pie crusts and apple peels and old cooked crook-necked squash in the trough.

4

What a great breakfast!

Maybe this isn't so bad, after all, thought the pig as he tucked in.

Mr. Quigley, one foot on the wall, nodded approval. "Yup," he said. "That's the way. Eat up, boy. Put more pork on those bones. Couple of months, you're going to be the best barbecue in the state."

The pig stopped eating. He blinked. Barbecue? *Me?* he cried. But the farmer only heard a regular pig squeal.

"Eat up, eat up," he said. "Enjoy it! Tomorrow I'm fixing to make you into a barrow, because barrows make smacking sweet eating. It's the barbecue that's important, boy." Off he went, bucket clanking, humming a tune.

The pig flopped into his wallow and rolled his eyes in despair.

A barrow! Him, a fine great boar, even if he didn't have his tusks yet, to become a barrow! He recalled another boar from way back who had been fixed this way so he'd never father a litter of piglets, or even have a mate. Not that this pig had a mate now, and he certainly did not like piglets. They made a racket and fought with one another and grew up to be big and push their father away from the trough. But to be a *barrow*!

"It's the *idea* of the thing," he groaned.

What should a pig who was sick of his pen, about to become a barrow tomorrow and a barbecue in a month or two, *do about it*?

"I shall have to change my identity completely," he said to himself. "No more of this idle dreaming. This is the time for action! I shall have to run away and begin a new life, as anything but a pig. Only not a chicken."

All day, while the sun ran its course, and at night while the clouds pushed past the moon, he puzzled over his problem. Wondering, pondering.

In the morning, while it was still dark, Mr. Quigley appeared, carrying a lantern and the bucket with a bigger-than-usual breakfast to spill into the trough. The pig came out of his house and nibbled a little, pretending to eat. Mustn't do aught to arouse suspicions. But the beans and the bread and—what was this? a whole baked apple!—were as sawdust in his mouth.

Mr. Quigley, naturally unaware of his pig's plans ("A pig have plans for himself! Ha-ha!"), patted his porker on the rump and said in a jolly way, "Get around to *you* late this morning. Enjoy your grub!"

"Enjoy your grub," the pig said to himself bitterly. He hated that word *enjoy*. If he were a man, he'd never tell anyone to "enjoy his grub," all the while planning to make a picnic out of him.

If he were a man!

A man. A man?

Well, why not a man?

Nobody told a *man* what to do. Nobody kept him pent in a pen. *Or* put a saddle on him, or whistled him to heel, or chopped off his silly chicken head.

Nobody barrowed and barbecued a man.

He made his decision. A man it would be. Next question: how to go about it? For an animal with his brains, there had to be an answer.

Putting his front feet on the trough, he looked over the wall. There was a light on in the farmhouse kitchen, and in the barn the farmer was milking by lantern light.

Dawn was coming up behind the hills. Chickens up; cat going home from the night's proceedings; no sign of dog or horse.

At the near side of the garden was the clothesline. The pig's eyes brightened. Putting one powerful shoulder against the gate of his pen, he shoved. Shoved some more. And, after a thoughtful pause, shoved more, a good deal harder. The gate refused to yield. Backing up to the farthest corner of his pen, he ran at the gate, head down between his shoulders. This time it gave a little. After three further assaults, it ripped from its hinges with a loud grating sound and fell away.

With a troubled glance at barn and farmhouse (would the farmer or his wife have heard? No, apparently not), he trotted over the gate, across the barnyard, onto the dewy grass, to the clothesline. There he pulled down a checkered shirt, a pair of pants, and a painter's hat. There was a blue bandanna, so he knotted that around his neck, as he'd seen Mr. Quigley and his sons knot theirs.

There he was—dressed!

He couldn't see himself, but it felt right.

"Now I am a man," he said aloud. "And a good choice, too."

He started off, and tripped on his shirt.

This won't do, he decided. I shall have to walk on two feet. Like the other men.

That wasn't so hard, except going downhill, when he had to run to keep up with himself.

On he went. The sun rose as he hurried to get away from Quigley's farm. And now, a strange thing happened. Walking upright, wearing a man's clothing, he found

that he was *feeling* like a man. He was thinking in human words, not in pig.

As he trotted along, thinking about this change and what it meant to him, he saw a man come out of a house beside the road. He was carrying a toolbox that he put in the back of his truck. Then he walked around to the front to turn the crank.

Well, thought the pig. I might as well find out right now if this idea is going to work. He walked up to the man and said boldly, "Howdy."

The man grunted something that could have been taken for a greeting.

Oh, *good*, thought the pig. He doesn't suspect. He said, "Hot, isn't it? A real porker. I mean, scorcher."

"I take it you want a ride," said the man, straightening up.

The pig had not had that in mind, but it seemed a good idea. "I do, yes," he said. "If it's not too much trouble."

"You crank, I'll get in and start the motor."

"All right," said the pig, and he seized the crank and gave it a few powerful turns.

"Well, get in, get in," said the man. "Whatcha waiting for?"

The pig hopped in the passenger seat. The man pulled out the choke, pumped the accelerator, shifted gears, and they rattled off down the road.

Easy as pie, thought the pig with elation. Why didn't I think of this ages ago?

"Name's Wheatley," said the man. "Henry Wheatley. What's yours?"

"My what?"

Mr. Wheatley frowned. "Your name. You got a name, don't you?"

"Oh, sure. Of course. Every man has a name. Who doesn't know that?"

"Well? What's *yours*?"

The only name the pig could summon to mind was Quigley, and he couldn't use that. He wanted to get as far from that as he could. Old Barbecue Quigley was not going to track him down that easily, by golly.

"Say listen, young fellow . . . you got something to hide?"

"What?" squealed the pig. "Me? Have something to *hide*? Ha-ha-ha . . . what a funny idea. Me! Something to hide! That's a good one, all right." He chuckled. "What gives you *that* idea?"

"What gives me the idea, young fellow, is that you won't give me your name. Something's funny, all right. I pick you up out of the kindness of my heart," he said crossly, "and you won't tell me your name."

"Oh, I don't mind giving you my name. Why should I? Easiest thing in the world, giving you my name—"

"*So?*" Mr. Wheatley began to apply the brakes.

"Quig—Quentin," the pig blurted. Was he laying a trail, using the horse's name? Why hadn't he thought one up before he started? Mr. Quigley, who'd given a name to his horse and a name to his dog, hadn't bothered giving such a—such a *permanent* thing to his pig. Something else to hold against him.

"Quentin *what*?"

They were passing a cornfield, and the pig said desperately, "Quentin Corn. That's it. That's my name. Quentin Corn. Everybody calls me Q. Just Q." Blur the tracks, that was the idea. Who'd associate a young fellow like him, going by the name of Q, with an escaped boar who'd only just missed being a barrow?

"Darndest name I ever heard of. Quentin Corn. Call you Q, do they. Never heard the like." But Mr. Wheatley speeded up a little and they rumbled on to town.

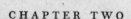

CHAPTER TWO

Mr. Wheatley pulled up to the side of a feed and grain store. It had a red and gold sign above the door, but Q found he couldn't read it. That was bad. He'd already come to expect that his human clothes would endow him with all human capabilities. He would have to do something about this if he planned to remain in the community of men. At the moment, though, he couldn't think just what.

Backing up to a side platform, Mr. Wheatley turned to his passenger and said, "Want to earn two bits, young fellow?"

"Two bits of what?"

Mr. Wheatley scratched his head. "Seems to me you're not quite bright. You sure you should be out on your own?"

Not bright! thought the pig. Who does he think he is, telling me, a pig, that I'm not bright? Recollecting, he said to himself sternly, "*Not* a pig! I'm a man, a man, a man." Maybe, as *men* went, he was not so smart yet. He had these *gaps*. He said humbly, "I've been living sort of out of the way. Sir," he added. That was what Mr. Quigley's sons called him. Perhaps young fellows were supposed to say it to grown-up men. "I'm not used to city talk."

"City?" said Mr. Wheatley, looking around his town. There was a village green with a Civil War cannon in the middle and a pump over a watering-trough for horses. Around the green were about twenty houses, a grocery, a livery stable with a gasoline pump to one side (combining the old and the new ways of getting about), a dry goods store with the post office inside, a house with a doctor's shingle at the gate, and this feed and grain store. At the far end of the green was a white wooden church with a lacy belfry and a fine house beside it.

"Some city," said Mr. Wheatley, but not without pride. "Two bits, son, is *city* talk for twenty-five cents. You want to earn twenty-five cents or don't you?"

That, the pig knew, was money. During his time in the pen he'd become an eavesdropper. When the farmer and his family and their friends strolled about on summer evenings, talking of this and that, the pig had listened closely, having little in the way of other entertainment. He'd picked up a lot of information about human beings that way, and one thing he'd definitely picked up was that money was *important*. Mr. Quigley and his family and his friends talked about it a very great deal. Clearly it was up to Q to find it important, too.

"I'd like it mighty well to earn two bits," he said to Mr. Wheatley.

"Well, you just unload those sacks of feed in the back of the truck there. Pile them—neatly, mind—right over

---

13

there at the side of the storeroom, *well* away from the doors, understand? I'm just going to step around home for my lunch. Back in about half an hour. That should give you plenty of time." He walked off, heavy-footed.

Q went around to the back of the truck and looked and was horrified. He hadn't noticed all these gunnysacks before, and he didn't see how, in half an hour, he was going to get them transferred from the truck to the side of the storeroom *well* away from the doors. Thinking it over, he realized that he'd never done a lick of work in his life before.

Still, as a man—or a young fellow, as Mr. Wheatley kept calling him—he was going to need money. Remembering those talks on the farm on summer evenings, he wondered if he wasn't going to need it more than anything else. Something he should have thought of, maybe, before deciding to be a man.

"Oh, *oink*," he said to himself, and set to work.

He found his great strength so equal to the task that he'd finished piling the grain sacks before Mr. Wheatley returned. He was sitting on the edge of the platform, wondering where he'd get his own lunch (*why* hadn't he eaten that last troughful before making his break for freedom and manhood?), when Mr. Wheatley appeared, looking content, as anyone, man or pig, looks after a good meal. Q was coming to the conclusion that a look of contentment was not Mr. Wheatley's usual expression.

"What d'ya know," he said. "Done already."

"You told me to get it done," Q said, somewhat sourly.

"I was halfway kidding. You must be a man of iron."

"It was nothing," Q grunted.

"You got a job, young fellow?"

"No." No job, no lunch. His stomach rumbled.

"Tell you what—fellow as strong as you—I'll give you a job as my helper. Pay you four bits a day, Sundays off, no pay. That's three dollars a week. Can't say fairer than that."

Q didn't know if he could say fairer than that. But he'd already decided that from now on he was going to have to work for what he ate, and *that*, to his mind, was fairer than being a barrow fed for nothing.

"All right," he said.

If Mr. Wheatley thought his new helper surly, he didn't comment. Nor did he inquire further about where the young fellow had come from. Plenty of them on the road these days. And New England people are not naturally curious, and sparing of words themselves. It was all right with Mr. Wheatley if Q, as he called himself, was sparing of them too.

"Muscle and stick-to-itiveness, that's what I want in a helper," he said.

"What do I help you do?"

Mr. Wheatley turned out his hands. "I'm the town handyman. Do anything—anything *legal*, that is, ha-ha—I'm paid to do." Lunch, thought Q, had certainly put his new boss in a good humor, which was more than Q was in. "Now we got this grain delivered," Mr. Wheatley went on, "I gotta get over to the rectory. I'm painting it." He rubbed his hands together and nodded with satisfaction. "Be a big help, having a strong young fel—"

"I'm hungry," said Q.

"Huh? Oh, well. Acourse, acourse. Perfectly natural. All right, Q, as you call yourself, here's your two bits—

overpaying, mind, but it's a one-time thing *this* time. You just go and get yourself some grub. Be quick about it."

"Where do I go to get it?"

Mr. Wheatley slapped his thigh. "Keep forgetting you just got here. Well, lessee. You gotta eat, and you gotta have a place to stay. That'll be Mrs. Benway's. She takes roomers. Salt of the earth, Mrs. Benway. Nice clean place. Sets a mighty good table. Yup. Mrs. Benway's your answer."

Q, by now half mad with hunger, said faintly, "Can I get some slops—some *grub* there? Right *now*?"

Mr. Wheatley scowled. "You won't be calling Mrs. Benway's food slops after you've tasted it. *Fine* thing. Slops."

"I'm *sorry*!" Q wailed. "It's just that I'm so hungry!"

"Well, get in the truck, we'll go on out there. Come along, come along. I gotta get over to the rectory before the moon comes up. . . ."

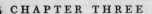

CHAPTER THREE

Mrs. Benway's rooming house was built of white clapboard, had a veranda running along the front with a trellis at one end, and carpenter's lace where pillars and roof joined. There was a porch swing, a rocker, several straight-back chairs companionably arranged, and some Boston ferns in wicker baskets. In the front yard was a circular garden of geraniums and petunias with a stone birdbath in the middle. All of this was surrounded by a low picket fence entwined with blue morning glories.

As a pig, Q had had an eye for the works of Nature, and he found his man's eye even more appreciative. If he had not been in such a rage for food, he would have stopped to examine and exclaim. As it was, he just hurried up the porch steps after Mr. Wheatley.

The woman who came to the screen door was fat, flushed, and cheery. She wore spectacles and had a turned-up nose and wiry gray hair. Altogether, in Q's view, she had a charmingly piglike appearance. He took to her at once.

"This here's Quentin Corn, my new helper," said Mr. Wheatley. "He's looking for lodgings."

"Right now I'm looking for lunch," said Q.

Appearing to find this funny, Mrs. Benway laughed.

"No, but seriously—" Mr. Wheatley began.

"I *am* serious," Q interrupted.

Mr. Wheatley frowned. "Let me do the talking, young fellow."

Just let me do the eating, thought Q. He'd never gone this long without food in his life before, and he wondered if he should be feeling faint. Was that a touch of dizziness in his head? Were their voices getting dim in his hearing?

"Why don't we talk in the kitchen?" said Mrs. Benway. Q revived at once.

The kitchen was all that a pig-become-a-man could dream of. Large black cast-iron stove with curlicue nickel decorations and a bracing odor wafting from it. At the back of the stove, on a rack, loaves of new-baked bread. Through an open pantry door he could see shelves stocked with jars of fruits and vegetables and preserves. A big wooden table almost white from many scrubbings had upon it a bowl of peaches and bananas and dark cherries.

"Just sit yourself down, young Quentin," said Mrs. Benway, hustling to the pantry and back. "How would some nice cold pork pie suit you?"

"Pork pie?" said Q, and now he did feel faint. "Pork?"

"You haven't tasted anything till you've had some of Mrs. Benway's pork pie," said Mr. Wheatley. "Unless it's her ham and split pea soup, which I had the pleasure of having some of the other evening."

No just split pea without ham? Q wondered. How

was he going to eat if all he got offered was food that would make him a cannibal? His dilemma was extreme, and without planning it he heard himself cry out, "Ma'am, I'm a vegetarian!"

Where had the inspiration come from? He did not know, but found Mr. Wheatley frowning at him much more seriously than he had frowned till now. Surely there were men who were vegetarians? Hadn't he heard a fellow, on one of those summer evenings, speak of being a—

"A vegetarian," Mr. Wheatley said irritably. "Well! I have never, not personally, been acquainted with a vege-*tar*ian before." He made it sound a low practice.

Too hungry to be intimidated, Q said, "If I could have some of this fruit here, and some milk maybe? And maybe a piece of bread. Or a half a dozen pieces. And that's coconut pie on the sideboard, isn't it? If I could maybe have a piece of that?" If he didn't eat pretty soon, he was going to keel over on Mrs. Benway's nice clean kitchen floor.

"Well now, bless you," said Mrs. Benway. "You just take all the fruit and bread you want." She went to the pantry and returned with a blue marbled jug. "And all the milk and pie you want, too. How does a young boy keep up his strength, eating like that?"

"Don't you worry none about his strength," said Mr. Wheatley. "He's built like a brick chimney. That's why I'm taking him on, bad manners and all. Why, thank you, Ada," he said, as she put a piece of pie and a cup of coffee in front of him.

"What's the matter with his manners, Henry? He's eating dainty as you please."

"Turning down your pork pie! Downright rude. This coconut pie is just about the best I ever ate, Ada."

"Oh, go on with you. I don't know what happened to the crust. I just don't have a light hand with it."

"Any lighter, we'd be setting on the clouds to eat."

"Oh, my," said Mrs. Benway, casting her eyes down. She looked up and said, "The lad wasn't rude. He's just a vegetarian. My Uncle Jack was one, and he was strong as a horse too."

"So you'll take him on as a roomer? Pay attention here, Q."

Q, gulping milk, gazed at Mrs. Benway over the rim of his glass.

"Sure I will," said Mrs. Benway. "You know, some ways he puts me in mind of that uncle of mine. Jack Hogg, he was. We used to laugh at his— What's the matter there, Quentin? You're choking! Pound his back, Henry!"

"Crumb," said Q. "Just swallowed a crumb."

"You've swallowed a whole loaf," Mr. Wheatley pointed out.

"Leave him be, Henry Wheatley. Well, being a vegetarian and all, seems hardly fair to charge him full rates."

"We don't want favors," said Mr. Wheatley without consulting Q. "You charge what you do the schoolteacher. And that drummer, Hargraves."

"Well. Well, all right." Mrs. Benway turned to Q, who was finishing a large piece of coconut pie and feeling pleased with himself. Yesterday a pig in a pen, today a boarder at Mrs. Benway's along with a schoolteacher and a man who played drums. Who knew what tomorrow held for him?

"Three dollars a week, that'll be," his landlady was saying. "Room and board and hot water for a bath once a week. You can't have Friday or Saturday, those're taken. And not Sunday, of course. But any other evening you please. Sheets changed every two weeks, towels once a week, and make your own bed in between. No late nights, no loud noise. Breakfast at six, dinner at noon, supper at five-thirty . . . seconds, but no thirds." She looked at him kindly. "An exception now and then for growing boys." She stopped for breath.

"I've only got twenty-five cents," said Q sadly.

Mrs. Benway and Mr. Wheatley exchanged glances. "I'm paying him three dollars a week," said the latter. "Not in advance, acourse. Can't see my way to make it more. Not till he proves himself. He has to prove himself. If he can."

Mrs. Benway looked at the ceiling, looked at the floor, closed her eyes, opened them, fixed them on Q. "Pshaw," she said.

Q got to his feet, picked up his hat, which he'd been sitting on, and said, "Thank you for lunch, ma'am. It was very very good. I would like to pay you with this two bits, if you please." He took the quarter from his shirt pocket and offered it to her.

"Got as good manners as the schoolteacher, I declare," said Mrs. Benway. "As for that drummer—you'd think *he'd* been brought up in a pigsty."

Q sat down again. He really wasn't up to these constant jolts.

"Tell you what, young Quentin," said Mrs. Benway, not noticing that Q was breathing jerkily, "tell you what.

You can have it, all found, for two dollars a week and chores."

"Now, I call that handsome," Mr. Wheatley exclaimed. "Downright generous. What's a few chores?"

Thinking he was asking to find out, Mrs. Benway said, "Just regular chores. Bring in the stove wood, after splitting it, empty the ashes, beat the carpets, weed the garden, mow the lawn, clean the lamp chimneys. Come fall and winter a few things besides, of course. Just chores."

"There now, Q. What d'ya say to that? A dollar off for helping around the house a little in your spare time."

Spare time? Q wondered.

"Speak up, speak up!" said Mr. Wheatley.

"Thank you, ma'am," said Quentin Corn. "You're very kind."

"I declare," said Mrs. Benway. "I don't know where you come from, and it's not my business to poke my nose in somebody else's, but they certainly taught you pretty manners, wherever it was."

A pigsty, ma'am, said Q to himself. Born and bred in a pigpen.

As for his manners, he didn't know where he'd got them. They seemed to have arrived when he'd garbed himself as a man. As, anyway, a boy. All in all, Q considered he'd made a good start toward being one or the other.

CHAPTER FOUR

The rectory, where the Reverend Wendell Emerson lived with his wife and three daughters, had been built next to the church in the eighteenth century. Both were the pride of the parish, and at a recent meeting of the elders it had been voted that the rectory was in need of painting. It was here that Mr. Wheatley and his new helper arrived in the early afternoon to begin work.

"We'll get this stuff out of the truck first," Mr. Wheatley directed. "Hop up there and hand me down the burlap first and then we'll stack the paint cans to the side here and— What're you waiting for? Move, *move!*"

Q scrambled into the back of the truck and pushed the length of burlap to the ground, handed the cans of white paint to his boss, the bucket of brushes, the gallon of turpentine, and a pile of rags.

"Now, here's what we do. As you can see, I've already done the scraping, so we'll just lay this burlap over the bushes—can't spatter Mrs. Emerson's bushes—and then

I'll do the painting. You had any experience painting, son?"

"No."

"Well, it's a particular job. You can start your apprentice work when we do a barn, something like that."

This was agreeable to Q, who was sure of his brawn but did not feel equal to anything "particular."

"You can hand me stuff as I need it, and clean the brushes and help me move the ladder when I need you. Meanwhile, no point you idling around, so as soon as we get the burlap laid, you go in and ask Mrs. Emerson what you can do to help her between-times."

"Right in the house?" Q asked nervously. He was meeting too many people all at once and would have been pleased to be spared further encounters.

"Acourse. You *been* in a house before, haven't you?"

Only one, thought Q. He said, "Ha-ha," indicating that he'd been going in and out of houses all his life. "Acourse."

"Then go around the side there to the kitchen door and ask Mrs. Emerson can you fetch or carry something— go, *go.*"

Q trotted around the path leading to the back of the rectory, and then sat on the back porch steps wondering what he'd got into and if he shouldn't, right now, try to get out of it.

He could run away again. But what then? Suppose next time he ran into a farmer? So far, these city people had taken him for what he claimed to be. They thought him pretty green, he knew that. He'd seen Mr. Wheatley tap his forehead and nod at Mrs. Benway, all but saying, "Young fellow's loopy." But a farmer, now. A farmer might not take him for a strong dumb lad. A farmer would probably ask himself what was that good-looking brown boar doing all duked up in a man's clothes. A farmer would probably take one look and say to himself, "*There's* a great barbecue if I ever saw one."

Q sighed and got up and knocked timidly at the door.

A little girl carrying a basket peered through the screen and began to laugh. "Look at you—you—*you*," she said, giggling. "*Look* at you! I *never* saw a pig in a painter's hat before! And a checked shirt! And pants and a nice neck-scarf! Oh, you look so *funny*! You look marvelous! You look—oh, I have to go *tell* somebody! This is *so funny*!"

"*Wait*! Wait, please," squealed Q. "Oh, please do wait, don't go tell somebody, little girl—"

She had started away, but turned back. "My goodness," she said seriously. "You talk. I *never* knew pigs could talk."

"No, no, no. I'm not a pig. Ha-ha-ha. That's funny. A pig! I'm a strong dumb lad who's working for Mr. Wheatley. Maybe I look like—but the fact is—"

"You—are—a—pig," said the little girl. She came out on the porch. The screen door slammed behind her, and they stood close together, each studying the other carefully.

"I guess I better run away again," said Q at length.

"Don't do that. I didn't mean—I mean, I'm sorry I laughed at you. That wasn't polite. But I thought it was a *joke*."

"Not to me, it isn't," said Q. "I stole these clothes and ran away from Mr. Qui—from the farmer, on the farm where I was, because Mr. Qui—he, the farmer, I mean, was going to make me into a barrow and a barbecue, one after the other, and I didn't take to the idea."

"My goodness, no. That's a terrible idea. You're such a *nice*-looking pig. Who'd want to eat you? Oh, I'm sure you'd *taste* good—I wouldn't want to insult you—" Emily said.

"Please," Q said weakly. "Don't talk like that."

"Tell me the rest. You ran away. When?"

"This morning," Q said dully.

"How did you meet Mr. Wheatley?"

"He picked me up in his truck, and then because I'm so strong he said he'd give me a job and he took me out to Mrs. Benway's and she says I can board there for two dollars a week and *chores*, and they don't know I'm a pig. They don't think I'm very smart—"

"I think you are *very* smart," said the little girl.

"I didn't fool you. Probably I won't fool anybody except Mr. Wheatley and Mrs. Benway. Maybe they just don't have good eyesight. Or maybe," he added, "*they* aren't too smart."

"I think," she said thoughtfully, "that you'll probably fool everybody but me. You're really very convincing."

By now they were sitting on the steps. The girl put her basket down, put her elbows on her knees, her chin in her hands. Q did likewise, and they sat there talking.

"Why should I fool everybody but you?" he asked. "How do you know so much?"

"I'm precocious."

"What's that?"

"Same as unmanageable."

"Oh." He nodded. "I see."

The girl turned and looked him in the eye. "Do you believe everything people say to you?"

"Shouldn't I?"

"My goodness, no. You'll never get away with it if you keep *that* up."

"Why do people say things they don't mean?"

"Well. *Some*times to be polite. Sometimes just to tease. Be *silly*. Like—precocious doesn't really mean unmanageable. I *can* be, of course. Unmanageable. But that's not what it means. It means I'm smarter than practically anyone else my age. But I couldn't *say* that."

"Why not?"

"It sounds like boasting. For instance, would you say out loud what a handsome pig you are?"

"If somebody asked me. I *am* handsome."

The little girl looked impressed. "For a pig, you're *beautiful*. But *people* don't say what's good about themselves. They tell their faults. Not big ones, see. Little ones. Expecting nobody'll believe them, of course."

Pretty disheartened, Q said, "I don't understand all this."

"It's easy. Now, my sisters—they're both much older than me—when their beaux come to take them somewhere—"

"Where?"

"Different places. A band concert, or a sociable. In winter a sleighride. That sort of thing. Well, if Augusta and Sophy are going out and they come into the parlor where the beaux are waiting and *they* get up and say, 'Oh my, you do look a treat, Augusta.' Or Sophy. Then *they* say, 'You're just *saying* that! I look a fright my hair's impossible and pink just is *not* my color . . . ,' or something like that, so then the beaux have to say that pink is just their color and their hair is scrumptious and—well, that's how it goes. See?"

Q shook his head.

The girl pondered. "My mother," she said. "She is a marvelous cook, and she knows it, too. But every single day when my father says, 'My dear, you've outdone yourself. These biscuits are *puffs* of pleasure,' or whatever he's making compliments about, Mama says, 'Oh, Wendell, they aren't . . . they're heavy today I don't know I just don't have the hand with biscuits I used to have—'"

"That's what Mrs. Benway said about her piecrust. She said she didn't have the *hand* with it, and Mr. Wheatley said she did, too. And she said, 'Oh, go on with you'—"

"Well, see?"

"It seems dumb."

"Lots of things are dumb about us. You'll find that out, all right, if you go on being a human person instead of a pig. But there are nice things, too."

"You're nice."

"I know."

"Aren't you supposed to say, 'Oh, I'm *not*, you're just *saying* that'?"

"See how fast you catch on? No, but I'm different. Being precocious."

"I see," said Q.

And he did see. What he found most difficult about his new role was the way he knew some things without trying to know them—like speaking man's tongue and having proper table manners and understanding what this nice girl was talking about, after she'd explained it a couple of times—but other matters were puzzles. Like not knowing about money. Or how to read.

"Hey, you! Q! What're you doing, setting there?" yelled Mr. Wheatley, coming around the corner of the house. "Oh, hello, Emily. See you've met my new helper."

"Hello, Mr. Wheatley," Emily said, getting up. "Yes, I have. We were just talking."

"Well," said Mr. Wheatley. He went on in a pleasanter tone, "I don't pay him to sit around talking, not even to you, Emily. I sent him around to ask your Mama if he could help out a bit till I need him."

Emily got up with her basket. "He can help me pick currants. We're going to make jelly."

"Just so's he makes himself useful. Come around front and help me with the ladder, Q, then hustle back here and get to work on those currants."

CHAPTER FIVE

It was a hot evening with trees massed blackly against a blue and pink sky, leaves motionless in the quiet air. There was an occasional passing car, or a horse and buggy. Lights were on in houses across the way. Millions of insects hummed and chirped in the dry grass. Large silver clouds, rose-tipped, moved across the sky like softly stirring animals.

"Wish those clouds meant something," said Mrs. Benway, moving a paper fan lazily in front of her perspiring face and neck. "No rain in I don't know when." The porch swing creaked as she pushed it slowly back and forth with her foot. A train whistle, deep-toned and wavering, sounded from beyond the hills. "The *State of Maine*," said Mrs. Benway. "Carrying all those people to fancy places. Oh my."

They were sitting on the veranda after supper. Mrs. Benway. Mr. Scott, the schoolteacher. Quentin Corn. Q had helped with the dishes, watching carefully everything that

33

was done, as he had been listening closely, all day, to everything that was said.

A large pot of water filled from the pump at the kitchen sink had simmered at the back of the stove while they ate. After supper, Mrs. Benway filled a basin, vigorously shook soap in a wire holder until she had the water frothing, then plunged the dishes and glasses in and scrubbed them, putting them in another basin of fresh hot water from which Q, wincing, plucked them, using a large white towel for drying. No one would have guessed that before this evening he'd never dried a dish, eaten at a table, or had a landlady. He did it all as if to the boardinghouse, and not to the pigpen, born.

Now, emboldened by Mrs. Benway's kindly gaze (she had never had a roomer offer to help in the kitchen before and didn't think drying dishes was part of a boy's chores), he decided to get into the conversation.

"I suppose he takes his drums with him," he said.

"Drums?" said Mrs. Benway. "Who takes his drums with him? What drums?"

"You said the other person who lives here, Mr. Hargraves, is a drummer. Does he take them with him when he's away? I just wondered."

Mr. Scott and Mrs. Benway laughed.

"Where *have* you been living?" she said. "Not that I'm asking, mind. I'm not one to pry. But a *drummer*. Everybody knows what a drummer is."

"I don't," said Q.

"A drummer is a salesman, Quentin," said Mr. Scott. He and Mrs. Benway did not call him Q, somewhat to Q's dismay. He didn't think he *had* to be dismayed. How could anyone connect either Q or Quentin—new helper of Mr. Wheatley, helpful boarder at Mrs. Benway's, and, as the opinion seemed to be, a stout if not brainy young *fellow*— with Quentin the horse, who lived on a farm far away where a pig had that very morning escaped certain death? No one, that was who.

Still, it was too bad they wouldn't say Q. Confuse the trail. If there was a trail.

"Why do they call him a drummer, if he's a sales-man?"

"He travels about drumming up sales."

"Oh. What does he sell?"

"Mr. Hargraves travels in ladies' corsets."

"He wears *corsets*?"

Again they laughed, even harder. Clearly he was not catching on to things now as well as he had earlier in the day. Well, he was tired. The whole day had been an adven-ture and he was tired out from having it.

"When you say a man travels in corsets, like Mr. Hargraves, or in biscuits or books or pots and pans, you mean that's what he's selling on his travels. You see?" said Mr. Scott.

Q saw. It seemed silly. Why not say Mr. Hargraves was a salesman who sold corsets?

Human beings are—complicated, Q said to himself, and he could not help marveling at how well he used words. Pigs are simple, and horses. Pigs are intelligent, and horses aren't stupid, but they are both *simple*. Chickens, of course, are dunces. But human beings are complicated. Tangled. *Confusing*.

Still, in one day he'd found himself getting fond of

them, not counting Mr. Quigley. He liked Mr. Wheatley in spite of his gruff ways, and Mr. Scott, who was skinny and serious. He very much liked Mrs. Benway and her good food and pretty piggy face. He positively doted on Emily.

For hours, it seemed, they had picked currants in the hot prickly sun, Emily telling him all sorts of things she considered he had better know.

"For instance," she'd said, "you've never been a boarder before."

"In a way, I was."

"But not in a *room*."

"The pen was pretty roomy."

"Q. *Pay* attention. You didn't have—well, a *bed* in your pen."

"No. Straw, of course."

"At Mrs. Benway's, you'll have a bed. Be sure you sleep on it."

"What did you think I was going to do?"

"I sort of had this idea you might lie down on the floor."

The two of them had laughed, the way Mrs. Benway and Mr. Scott now laughed over his mistake about the drummer in corsets. Laughing, Q thought, was just about the best part of being human.

The landlady and her roomers sat watching the rose tint fade from the sky as darkness came on. The hum of the insects became a roar. Bats whisked past the streetlights and moths began to flutter against the screens, attracted by the glow of a kerosene lamp in the front room.

Dr. Anthony went by in his Model T, tooted and waved

but did not stop. He left a cloud of dust behind him that settled slowly back on the road.

"He's a good man," said Mrs. Benway.

"He is," said Mr. Scott.

For a while there was no traffic. Then a policeman rode slowly past on his bicycle, slowed a bit at Mrs. Benway's gate, put two fingers to his helmet in greeting, and pedaled steadily out of sight.

"That's Constable Mears," Mrs. Benway told Q. "Such a nice man. Poor as Job's turkey. Town doesn't pay him enough. Of course, he gets his house. Such as it is." Her brow wrinkled slightly. "Mr. Scott?"

"Yes, Mrs. Benway?"

"*Did* Job have a turkey? I've been hearing that expression all my life, but I just thought—I don't recall anything about a turkey in the book of Job. In the Bible anywhere, come to that."

"Now, that's a very interesting question, Mrs. Benway. I remember oxen and camels and she-asses and sheep. And the young lions, of course. But a turkey? Did they even have turkeys in Job's day? Probably it's a generalization. After all, everything connected with Job was in poor shape for a while."

"That must be it."

Q listened to their voices sleepily . . . he thought he'd better go in and snuggle on his bed of straw . . . this cackle in the yard was keeping him awake . . . geese gabbling? turkeys gobbling? . . . softer sounds, maybe . . . but he was getting very very sleepy and had better get out of the wallow . . . into his house . . . onto his straw . . .

Mr. Scott slapped his knees and got up from the steps,

where he'd been sitting with his back against the railing. "Off to bed. Have to catch the seven o'clock bus."

"Summers," Mrs. Benway explained to Q, "when school doesn't keep, Mr. Scott does bookkeeping at the bank over to the county seat, so other people can have their days off."

"That's nice," Q said groggily.

"I don't do it to be nice, Quentin," said Mr. Scott. "I do it to keep eating Mrs. Benway's good cooking, and sleeping on her fine bed. That's the hardest part of this summer job. I don't get home for noonday dinner."

"Now, now, Mr. Scott. I've packed you a good lunch for tomorrow, with a surprise in it."

"Oh, I'm not complaining. Your lunchbox is a treat. Only I never can decide if I'd rather teach school than bookkeep because I like to teach school, or because then I get back for dinner every day. Well, 'night, both of you. Pleasant dreams."

He went in, beating away the moths before he opened the door, then closing it quickly behind him.

"Fine young man," said Mrs. Benway, who seemed to like everybody. She got heavily to her feet. "He always calls this *home*. Actually, he comes from Massachusetts. We were lucky to get him for the school. Well, let's go in, Quentin. Mind the moths."

Quentin Corn, climbing the stairs to his room, carrying his bed-candle, thought that he, too, would like to call this "home." Maybe one day, if he was lucky, if he was careful, if Mr. Quigley didn't catch up with him and nobody here in town except Emily caught on to him, maybe one day he'd be able to.

CHAPTER SIX

It was Saturday. Nearly a week had passed since Q had arrived in the town. Except for a few minor problems and one major one (he could neither read nor write and it was *distressing*), he was adapting to his human condition as if he'd always known it and no other.

"Quentin," said Mrs. Benway after breakfast, "before Mr. Wheatley comes for you, fill the birdbath like a nice boy. How the poor things find anything to drink, far less bathe in, the Dear only knows. I declare, if it doesn't rain soon I'm going to dry up and blow down the road like a leaf."

"Me, too," said Q.

Mr. Scott, home for the day, looked at the two of them, so solid and stout, and smiled. "Well," he said, "if you will excuse me, I'll be on my way." He took up a fishing pole and tackle box from the porch floor.

"You didn't ask me to pack a lunch, Mr. Scott!" cried Mrs. Benway.

"No need, no need." He smiled even more broadly. "Augusta is going fishing with me, and she is providing the picnic basket." He walked away down the street, humming to himself.

"They're keeping company, you know," said the landlady, looking after him with approval.

"Keeping who company?" asked Q.

She shook her head. "You are such an innocent, Quentin. They're walking *out* together, he and Augusta Emerson. A nicer girl you couldn't find, except Sophy perhaps."

"And Emily," Q said indignantly.

"Yes, of course. Emily is fine," she said, and added, "A bit harum-scarum *and* uppity for some people's taste. It's all very well, Quentin, to be smarter than most, but a person shouldn't *show* it."

"How can she help showing it if she's smart?"

"She should hide her light under a bushel." Mrs. Benway patted him on the head, as if to say that the quality of cleverness was one that he, Quentin, need not trouble himself about. In less than a week he had come to be accepted as a good lad with very little brain, and Emily had said he should keep things that way.

"After you've been here a while," she had told him, "you can start being smart. Sort of creep up on them. Probably they won't even notice, but if they do they'll think it's because you've been living with a schoolteacher. And, of course, associating with *me*."

"Quentin Corn, are you listening to me?" Mrs. Benway demanded.

"I'm sorry. I was thinking about Emily."

"Now, Quentin," said Mrs. Benway merrily, "you leave that kind of thinking to Mr. Scott, who's old enough for it. You're nothing but a boy, and Emily's a little girl, for all she tries to talk like a college professor."

Q sighed. Again he didn't know what she was talking about. Or, he knew what she was saying, but had no idea what she meant by it. He was maybe bright enough for a pig, but as a human being he had *gaps*.

"Quentin, I want you to listen to me. Mr. Wheatley will be along soon. What I've decided is that since Mr. Hargraves writes he won't be back for another week, you can have your bath this evening when you get home from work. We want you all clean and tidy for church tomorrow."

Church? thought Q. Bath?

Every afternoon when he got back to his lodgings, he sluiced down at the pump in the back yard, lathering with a big bar of yellow laundry soap, then rinsing again in the cool rushing water that sprang from the pump as he worked the handle.

"Why do I have to take a bath?" he demanded. "I can wash at the pump."

"Pshaw. Just like a boy. No arguments, Quentin. When you get home we'll fill the washtub in the kitchen. I'll have water heating for you on the stove and—"

"In the kitchen? I'll be naked! Everybody can look!"

"Who wants to look at you, for goodness' sake? Besides, there's the two big screens that go around the washtub that we all use. Nobody's immodest in this house, let me tell you. And now—about your clothes. They're sweaty and dirty enough to walk by themselves—"

"That's all I have."

"So I have noticed. Don't think you fool me, Quentin. Because you don't, not for one minute. I know exactly what you are."

Q's vision blurred. His head reeled. "You do?" he quavered. "I don't? Fool you? You mean— But then why have you been pretending not to know that I'm a—"

"That you are a runaway boy? Well, I do know, and I haven't been pre*tend*ing anything. I just feel it isn't my place to poke and pry into a young fellow's reasons." She sighed hugely. "If you must know," she went on, oblivious to the fact that all Q knew was that he had been shaken to his marrow and was far from recovered, "if you must know —my own son, Pete, is a runaway. Fact is, that's his room you have now. That's how I could take you in, because his room is empty. Been empty for two years. He ran off when he was fourteen, and all I've ever heard from him is a post-card from Gloucester, Massachusetts. It said, 'Back some-day. Your son, Pete.'" She put a corner of her apron to her eyes, where large tears were forming. "I know that lads leave home everywhere these days and go on the road, but at least they could let a body *know*, once in a *while*—" She broke off and turned away with a small sob.

Q, feeling a little (not very) guilty about his decep-tion, but terribly sorry for nice Mrs. Benway, tried to think of a comforting word.

"Is that his nightshirt you left on the bed for me?" he asked at length. It wasn't the *most* comforting remark possible, but he was still not recovered from the shock of thinking himself found out.

It seemed to do the trick. Mrs. Benway was incapable of thinking about herself, even about her own troubles and sorrows, for long at a time. She blew her nose and nodded and said, "You're just about his size, Quentin, so I'm going to take these dirty duds of yours and they'll get a good scrubbing come Monday. And you'll wear Pete's good shirt and pants to church tomorrow, and his work-clothes after that. He did just what you did, ran off in nothing but the clothes he stood up in. I declare, boys don't *think*, they simply do not think. Well—" Another big sigh, then a little smile. "Here comes Mr. Wheatley now. Off with you, Quentin. Thought I'd make chicken fricassee and dumplings for dinner. Sure you'll eat chicken? Sort of funny, for a vegetarian."

"There are different degrees of strictness," said Q, quoting Emily. He'd explained to her how he'd dodged the pork pie. ("I can't eat pig, and I don't think I could choke down cattle, but a bit of *chicken* from time to time, that would be nice," he'd told her wistfully. The only use he could see at all for chickens was to eat them or their eggs.

"*Tell* her you'd like chicken, Q. She'll be delighted. Tell her there are different degrees of strictness in being a vegetarian, and chicken is inside your limits. And, Q— don't say pig and cattle. It's pork and beef.")

"Well, that's fine," said Mrs. Benway, quite back to her hearty self. It set her up, having something to cook that she knew was going to be praised. With dumplings, though it wasn't a thing she'd say aloud, she had the hand of an angel.

CHAPTER SEVEN

Instead of making the left turn at the green toward the church and rectory, Mr. Wheatley swung his truck to the right and they rattled past the livery stable, Macky's Feed & Grain, the dry goods store and post office, and Dr. Anthony's house. Behind the green, on a narrow lane, was a cottage, once white, now dingy, with a sagging porch, peeling paint, and a lot of broken or mended toys scattered around the small front yard. Scattered about the yard, too, was a horde of yellow-haired girls—playing, shouting, calling, shoving one another about, climbing the branches of the one tree, dashing in and out of the house through a broken screen door.

Q, who'd been one of a big litter himself, recognized a family when he saw it.

Mr. Wheatley stopped alongside the picket fence that had several palings gone and, like the house, was sadly in need of paint.

"Going to help Constable Mears this ayem," he said. "Prop up that porch before one of the youngsters breaks a leg or arm. Come along, come along, Q. Help me get these two by fours outa the back here. Step lively!"

The children, whose clamor had drowned even the arrival of Mr. Wheatley's rackety truck, were all at once alerted to his presence. They came pounding forward like a herd of ponies, bare feet thudding, voices shrill in greeting. They surrounded Mr. Wheatley, grabbing his arms, tugging at his shirt, leaping around him with shrieks of welcome.

To Q's surprise, Mr. Wheatley looked pleased. Grouchy Mr. Wheatley, who was always admonishing Q to "move, *move* . . . come along, come along . . . step lively there!," was smiling down at the children in the most— the most *genial* manner. (Nice word, genial. Emily said that's what her father was. "He's such a genial man," she'd said, adding, "A little bit lazy, but that's a family characteristic on my father's side. Sophy and I didn't inherit it, but Augusta did.")

There stood Mr. Wheatley, swarmed over by this litter, smiling as if he had all the time in the world. He began a slow progress toward the house, impeded by clinging girls and laughing heartily. "All right, now, all right, you bunch of imps . . . if you'll let me get a hand free, I'll—"

They fell away from him and stood looking into his face with happy expectancy as he took from the pocket of his carpenter's apron a sack of penny candies.

"You, Beth," he said to the oldest girl, "you see to the

distribution. It'll be high noon before I get started." He mounted the porch steps. "Come along, come along, Q. I want you to meet Mrs. Mears, the constable's wife." He stopped abruptly and said, "Pshaw. Lookit Andy, there."

At the end of the porch, sitting in a little chair just the right size for him, was a small child, yellow-haired like the girls but, unlike them, quiet. He was wearing a blouse and pants of black cotton, too large. He lowered his head and stared upward through his lashes at Mr. Wheatley. He had a wisp of a smile.

"Let me see, now," said the big man. "You *are* Andy, aren't you? Haven't got you mixed up with somebody else?"

A nod of the head, a shake of the head.

"Then it's just got to be your birthday. I'm right again?"

Another nod.

"And, lessee . . . you're exactly forty-three years old today. I'm right again, hey?"

The smile broadened to the real thing, and Andy held his closed fist in front of his nose, then lifted one, two, three fingers.

"Three!" exclaimed Mr. Wheatley. "Missed by forty whole years. I'll be goshed." He put a hand into the apron pocket again and took out a small carved wooden bird. The other children had gathered beneath the porch, which had no railing, to watch with pleasure. Andy's eyes widened, but he made no move toward the bird.

Mr. Wheatley squatted beside him. "Now, to the ordinary eye, which yours is far from, this does look like an ordinary whittled bird, don't it? But let me *tell* you—" He broke off and looked at Q. "Son, trot in and tell Mrs. Mears we're here to fix the porch. That's her sewing machine in there, going to beat the band. Well, move, move—"

"But—I don't know her."

"You don't have to know her. You only have to tell her. You can see I'm busy here. Introduce yourself, if you want to be formal. Go, go—" He turned back to Andy. "Besides being a bird, Andy, this here's a flute. Well, kind of. See this hole that's on the barrel, so to speak? Well, if you put your finger on and off it, and blow through this end . . . Let me show you." He put the wooden bird gently to his lips and blew a long sweet note, then fluttered his finger at the single hole on the reed and the note twittered.

Andy's chest lifted. He exhaled a long sigh. Still he did not reach for his present, seeming content to leave it in Mr. Wheatley's possession.

"Hmm," said Mr. Wheatley, looking baffled. "Look here, Andy. Remember when I made this here chair for you?"

A nod.

"Took you so long to sit down in it, I thought you'd be growed before you tried. Cast me down something awful, that did. Isn't that right, youngsters?" he asked his audience, who shouted in agreement. "Well, when you finally got around to squatting in it, seems like we won't ever get you out. Now, it's the same with this whittled bird. It's a present that I made for you with my own weary hairy hands and you have to take it or I guess I'll just be obliged to cry tears. Grown man like me. You want that to happen?"

Andy shook his head.

"Take it! Take it and blow on it, Andy!" shouted his sisters. "Before Mr. Wheatley is obliged to cry!"

Slowly, with many hesitations, Andy reached for the little flute and finally held it in his hands. Q, who had been watching breathlessly, went, "Poof!"

"Are you still here?" Mr. Wheatley demanded. "Thought I told you to tell Mrs. Mears—"

"All right. I'm going," Q said sullenly. He couldn't understand Mr. Wheatley. Of course, he knew his boss was a kind man. He'd helped Q from the minute they'd met that morning five days ago. But he was always so gruff, so nearly out of patience. Only it was beginning to seem that he was that way only with Q. Or was he *this* way only with the constable's children?

Mysterious mysterious creatures, Q said to himself. If he lived among them the rest of his life, he would never really understand them.

He knocked on the broken screen door. There was no response, so he stepped into a narrow hall and walked down it, toward the humming sound. Behind him he heard a little *tweet*, and could not help smiling. The only sound Andy had so far made.

Tweet!

In a room at the end of the hall, a woman with blond hair speckled gray leaned, with her back to the door, over a sewing machine. One foot rode the treadle and her hands guided a length of cloth under the needle. The room was entirely taken up with bolts of cloth and balls of trimming, with a wire dressmaker's dummy, with boxes of threads and ribbons and empty spools and buttons and papers of hooks and eyes and needles and pins. On the table were

some flour sacks. They had a picture of a little girl on them and the words, could Q have read them, *Hecker's Flour*. He realized that he had seen, on the girls out in the yard, dresses made out of these flour sacks.

Come to think of it, Mr. Quigley had used such sacks for storing corn in. Q thought making dresses out of them was nicer, and that Mrs. Mears must be very smart to think of it.

"Ma'am?" he said, lifting his voice above the whir of the machine. "Ma'am. I'm here to tell you we're here."

Mrs. Mears turned, brushed a strand of hair back, and said, "You're here to tell me who's here?"

"Mr. Wheatley and me. To fix your porch."

"Oh. Oh, dear." She got up, stretched her back, and said again, "Oh dear. Whatever would we do without Mr. Wheatley? Fixes the house, treats the children, never takes a dime. Oh, yes. We're indebted to Mr. Wheatley."

Q wondered if, since Mr. Wheatley didn't take a dime for working on this house, he himself would get his day's pay. He wouldn't ask, of course. But he did not want to get behind in his room and board. Though he did, in the evening, as many chores as he could, he never felt he was doing enough.

Mrs. Mears started down the hall, turned, and said, as if just now aware that she didn't know him, "Who are you?"

"Quentin Corn, ma'am. Mr. Wheatley's new helper."

"I see. The Dear knows he needs one. The way that man works . . . Mr. Wheatley! Hello! How did you know the porch needed fixing?"

"Well, Mrs. Mears, I happened to drive past the other

day and noticed it was leaning clean away from the house, and I said to myself, there's a porch needs fixing if ever I saw one . . ."

"What's that Andy has?" she interrupted. "Oh, now . . . Oh, will you just look at that. A whistle! A little whittled whistle that you made yourself, Mr. Wheatley. Seems I'm always thanking you for something. Andy, did you say thank you to Mr. Wheatley?"

He said *tweet*, thought Q.

"If I may ask, Mrs. Mears, why's the young fellow wearing black for his birthday? Gave me quite a turn when I saw him."

Mrs. Mears's hands flew to her face, and she flushed. "No hiding anything from you, is there, Mr. Wheatley?" she said, and Q heard a far-off tweet in her voice. Not a sweet tweet. Maybe a bitter tweet. "I made it out of the old umbrella that turned inside out on Mr. Mears during that last awful storm we had. It was *so* windy—I just don't recall such a wind. And since he couldn't fix it . . . Well, I couldn't let all that good cotton go to waste, could I?"

Mr. Wheatley was lunging about with embarrassment. "Mrs. Mears!" he said loudly. "Mrs. Mears, I don't know what come over me. That was a purely awful thing for me to—I mean, I can't think what come over me. And in front of the youngsters. I just can't say how sorry—"

"Never mind, Mr. Wheatley." Mrs. Mears lifted one hand and let it fall. "Nothing the youngsters don't know about making do."

"But I didn't mean—"

"You mean *well*, Mr. Wheatley. And well do I know it."

"Can't think what come over me," Mr. Wheatley grumbled, going down the steps to his truck. "Come along, here, Q. Hop to it, or we'll never get done."

But as the hours passed and they sawed and planed and nailed and propped, with the Mears girls as vocal and admiring onlookers and smallbore helpers (nail picking-up, hammer-handing), Mr. Wheatley became again good-humored, as Q had never seen him before today.

At mid-morning, Mrs. Mears came out of the house carrying two tall glasses of lemonade.

"Here you are, Mr. Wheatley," she said, with a little flourish. "Refreshment for you and the young fellow here."

"Well now, Mrs. Mears, there was no call for you to do that. We make out just fine with water, no need for you to—"

"Oh, but there is a need, Mr. Wheatley. I *need* to offer a small hospitality to people who are doing me such a kindness."

Mr. Wheatley took off his hat, rubbed his forehead with his forearm, and said, "Well, it's kind, and mighty welcome. *Right*, Q?"

"Oh, yes," Q said sincerely, gulping the cool tart drink. He paused for a moment to bob his head at Mrs. Mears. "It tastes wonderful."

"Why don't you two sit down for a spell?" she asked. "Even *hired* help gets to rest once in a while."

"I don't know that we should—" Mr. Wheatley began, then said hastily, "That's a *good* idea, Mrs. Mears. C'mon, youngsters. I'll tell you a story about my railroading days. You too, Q."

Q, exhausted from the unaccustomed work he'd been doing the past week (am I that pig, he wondered, who lay around with not one thing to do except get fat?), collapsed under a tree, leaning his back against it.

He closed his eyes. The sound of Mr. Wheatley's voice, and the children's voices, threaded through with the voices of birds and insects and the faraway hum of the sewing machine, began to mingle in a musical drone. His head fell forward.

"Tweet!"

His muscles jerked and he started heavily, then sank back, blinking. "It's you, Andy," he said. "You and your bird-flute. Guess I was almost asleep."

Andy, looking up from under his long lashes, fixed his bright blue gaze on Q's face for a while, and then, for the first time that morning, he said something.

"I didn't know pigs could talk," he said.

CHAPTER EIGHT

O h, my *goodness*, Q," said Emily. "What did you do? What did you *say*?"

"At first I was so surprised I hardly thought I was hearing right. I've got so used to being a runaway lad I sometimes practically forget I'm still a pig. And then I didn't know what to do. Or say. I just thought I'd have to run away again, and I guess maybe I better. What else can I—"

"You *mustn't*. Not yet. Not unless you're really found out. Andy Mears is about as wide-awake as anyone in this town, but he just about never says a *word*. Probably he won't say one now. I won't have you running away. We'll have to think of something to do about Andy."

"I did do something," Q said. "It might work."

"What?"

"I leaned over and said into his ear, *very* softly, practically not even a whisper, 'It's a secret, Andy. Can you keep a secret?'"

Emily looked vastly respectful. "Oooh. You are *so* smart, Quentin Corn. That was the perfect thing to say. Andy would rather keep a secret than—than see Saint Nicholas."

"Who's Saint Ni—"

"Never mind, Q. I'll tell you about that some other time. You think he agreed? I'm sure he did."

"He didn't say," Q replied, and they could not help laughing.

"He just about never does say. Anything. People think Andy is slow because he doesn't talk. But I think he's a fox. Never misses anything, stores it all up in that pretty head. He's biding his time, that's what I think."

"When it's all bided, what then?" Q asked glumly.

"Nothing bad. Never. I'm sure of that. He's a *good* little person. I just have a feeling that when he grows up he's going to be some important smart person who does *world-shaking* things. That's all."

It seemed a lot to Q, but if Andy planned to bide his time until he was grown up and important, it was too far away to worry about now. That was what was important to Q.

"So you do think he'll keep me a secret?"

"Sure of it, Q. But you see what I mean about him. He probably hasn't said fourteen words in two weeks, but when he gets around to talking he says something absolutely correct."

"The way you did," said Q.

"Just so. You see, you're perfectly safe. Andy and I are the smartest people in this town and we both intend to keep you our secret. So stop worrying."

All very well for her to say, but it seemed to Q that it would only take a word, even an accidental word, from Andy, whom he wasn't sure of, or an equally accidental slip on the part of Emily, of whom he was sure, to unmask him before the entire town. Once people looked at him with the word "pig" instead of "lad" in their minds, it would be all up with him and his new life.

Well, he comforted himself, there's always running away. I did it once, I can do it again. And again and again, if I have to.

He'd hate to leave Emily.

They were in the large kitchen garden behind the rectory, picking corn, hidden in the tall stalks. The ears were warm, the silken tassels fragrant. Grasshoppers sprang, birds sang. Oh, it would be hard to leave all this. And Emily.

Mr. Wheatley, having given the morning to Constable Mears's porch, had dropped Q at his rooming house, picked him up after a noonday dinner of chicken and lovely dumplings, and driven here to continue painting. Q had helped with the pails of paint, the turpentine and brushes and rags, had draped the bushes with burlap. Then he'd spent a couple of hours applying paint in broad strokes to the bottom boards behind the bushes. He could wriggle in there more easily than Mr. Wheatley, who had decided to trust him this much with the "particular" work.

Then Emily had come asking for help in picking corn. Mr. Wheatley, who couldn't seem to refuse children, had let him go.

Now, carrying the corn between them in a sack, they sat on the back porch to shuck.

"There you are, children," said Mrs. Emerson, coming to the kitchen door. "I'm going into the church to see to the flowers, Emily, and then I'm to join Sophy at Mrs. Macky's quilting. There's milk and cookies for you and Quentin when you've finished the corn. Remember, I want tomatoes and peppers and cucumbers ready when I get back. I plan to make a start on the relish this afternoon, with the assistance of the Guild ladies. A bushel of each, say."

"I won't be finished with all that till midnight," Emily said under her breath.

"Did you grumble something, Emily?" her mother asked.

"No, Mama. Not really."

"Good. When you're finished with your chores, and if Mr. Wheatley can spare him—only *if*, mind you—then you and Quentin are free to play."

As Mrs. Emerson walked across the garden path to the church, Emily made a face at her. "When you are quite finished working yourself to *death*, Emily, then you are free to *play*." She looked at Q. "Sophy over there gossiping and giggling among the patterns. Augusta off spooning with Mr. Scott. I ask you."

"Couldn't you go to the quilting?" Q asked, not suggesting she'd be welcome at the spooning.

"I hate sewing," she said cheerfully. "Sophy's always trying to get me to learn needlepoint. I told her I'm afraid of needles and I don't see the point. Wasn't that funny?"

"Oh, yes," said Q, not seeing the point either.

They finished shucking the corn and then Q said he'd better check with the boss before having milk and cookies.

"Quite the fair-haired boy around here, aren't you?" said Mr. Wheatley. "All right. I don't see why not. I'll give you a call if I need you. Don't make me call twice."

Sitting on a porch chair, eating gingerbread men and drinking milk cool from the icehouse, Q said thoughtfully, "Most of the time, Mr. Wheatley is sort of—sort of cranky with me. I don't know why. Not *very* cranky, but, just the same . . ."

"He's that way with everybody, Q. He's had disappointments, Mama says. He wanted to be a railroad man, but it didn't work out."

"He told the children he was an engineer on the *Boston and Maine*," said Q, who had heard that much through his drowsy stupor this morning.

"*Poor* Mr. Wheatley. No, he started on the railroad as a call-boy, but for some reason he got thrown off. And then the lady he wanted to marry didn't want to marry him and he never found one that did want to marry him that he wanted to marry, so he's lonely be*sides* being disappointed."

"He's awfully nice to the Mearses. Not cranky at all."

"Probably because he's always helping them somehow. Besides, he likes children, and Constable Mears has so many."

"*I'm* a *lad*," Q pointed out.

"Grown up enough to be his helper. That makes you different. And I think maybe he disapproves of you a little, because of being a runaway. It was Mrs. Benway, you know, who was the lady who didn't want to marry him, but she married Mr. Benway instead. Only now she's a widow, so she *could*, only she still doesn't want to. One day she was talking with my mother and Mama said, 'But Mr. Wheatley's a good man, Mrs. Benway, and you must be lonely after all these years,' and Mrs. Benway said, 'He's as good a man as a body could find, but he has a dark disposition and who knows but he might give *me* one?' So I guess she doesn't want to, but Mr. Wheatley wants to. And her son, Pete, ran away, so probably he thinks maybe you remind her of Pete and it might make her sad. But Q, he must like you just the same, because why give you a job and call you 'son' the way he does, if he doesn't? Come to think, maybe he thinks that if he helps you, someone else might help Pete, and Mrs. Benway would be grateful, although actually nobody else much likes Pete except his mother."

Q listened to all this attentively. "Why don't people like him?"

"Because—well, he's sly. Sort of mean. He just is not nice. Ran off and didn't even say goodbye and only has sent poor Mrs. Benway one measly postcard from Gloucester, Massachusetts, in all this time."

"Does everybody know everything about everyone in this town?"

"Pretty much. It's a *small* town, see. Probably I know more than most because I eavesdrop. It's one way to learn things they don't want you to know. One thing, Q, at least you didn't break some poor mother's heart when you ran off."

Q, who had an excellent memory, had none at all of his mother, and recalled his brothers and sisters without interest. The truth was, he'd never really got close to another pig, and now it looked as if he never would. "I couldn't write her a postcard anyway," he said. It was a constant vexation that with all that had come to him, like a gift, when he put on human clothes—speech, nice manners, a grasp of the functions of objects he had never seen before —somehow the ability to read and write had been left out.

"We'll work on that," Emily said confidently. "Tomorrow, after services, we'll start teaching you the alphabet." She jumped up, went in the house, and came out with a pad of paper and a pencil. "We'll start right now." Carefully she drew a large circle, then put a small curvy line at the bottom. "That," she said, "is your very own letter. It's a Q."

Q looked at the outline with a dreamy, rapt expression. It put him in mind of himself when young. Nice round body, little curly tail. They'd been happy ones, his piglet days. Too bad he'd had to grow up to be a boar. In spite of his present, pleasant position in man's world, he felt a moment's sharp longing for that other, earlier, lazier life.

"You try," she said. "Go on, Q."

He picked up the pencil and drew a careful perfect Q.

"There!" said Emily. "You'll be writing and reading in no time."

"Do you really think so?"

"I do, yes."

"Where is everybody?" said the Reverend Emerson, stepping out on the porch.

"You mean where is everybody *else*," Emily said. She waved her hands. "Gone, all gone. I only am escaped alone to tell thee."

Mr. Emerson gave a shout of enjoyment. "My Bible-spouting daughter, quoting *Job*."

"Papa, this is Quentin Corn. This is my father, Q, the very right Reverend Mr. Wendell Emerson, famously descended, though distantly."

Q got to his feet. "How do, sir."

"Well, well. At last I lay eyes on you. Emily talks of you from morn till night. But I think you and I might have a serious discussion soon, Quentin Corn."

Q's heart sank. The discussion, he had no doubt, would be about runaway boys and how to reform them. "Did Job have a turkey, sir?" he said, in an effort at diversion.

"Turkey?"

"You said Emily was quoting from *Job*, and Mrs. Benway and Mr. Scott were wondering if he had a turkey. Because Mr. Mears is poor as Job's turkey, Mrs. Benway said."

"My goodness," said the minister. "A turkey."

"There are oxen and camels and she-asses and sheep. And the young lions, of course," said Q, his good memory serving him nicely. "But they can't remember anything about turkeys."

"There isn't a mention of a turkey." Mr. Emerson sat down, took a cookie, cocked his head, and mused. "Eagles . . . *as the eagle that hasteth to the prey.* Owls. *I am a brother to dragons, a companion to owls.* Fowls. *Ask now the beasts, and they shall teach thee! and the fowls of the air, and they shall tell thee*: Chapter twelve, verse seven. Birds and beasts galore in *Job*, but no turkey. How interesting. Well, well—to work. I shall be in my study, dear," he said to Emily. "Working on my sermon."

"We'll be in the garden, gathering the sheaves," she said. "Anyway, the tomatoes and peppers and cucumbers."

He laughed again and gave her a hug. "Emily, Emily—my treasure past measure. I shall see you both again," he said, and went back into the house.

"Isn't he handsome?" Emily said. "Probably gone in to work on his snooze."

"Are you his favorite child?" Q asked.

"No, no. He loves us all. My father is philoprogenitive. Like Mr. Wheatley."

"Are you going to tell me what that means?"

"It means they like children. I do not believe in using simple terms, Q, when complicated ones will do just as well."

"I don't want to have a serious discussion with your father, Emily. I would hate it."

"Don't worry. I'll fix it."

"How?"

"Tell him you ran away from an orphanage. That'll be best. I'll tell him that you refuse to divulge its location because they would make *reprisals* against you if you were sent back, and we have to respect your wishes. Papa is really good at respecting children's wishes, which most grownups are not. Sometimes I do think it's because it's a lot easier not to meddle. Papa likes things to be easy and peaceful. But it comes out to the same in the end."

"Your mother won't want to have a talk with me, will she?"

"Goodness, no. She does what Papa does, and if he doesn't she won't."

"You there! Q!" Mr. Wheatley's heavy step was on the porch and there he stood, glaring. "Been calling you—"

"It was our fault, Mr. Wheatley," said Emily, jumping

up. "Papa's and mine. Papa and Q were having a Bible discussion."

"Oh." Mr. Wheatley looked nonplussed. "Well. In that case, of course. You know your Bible, do you, Q?"

"Hardly at all," Q said hastily.

"He's modest, Mr. Wheatley," Emily said.

"So I see. Well. All right, Q, come along and help me get the things in the truck. It's late in the day, and it's Saturday, and I'm tired."

"See you tomorrow after services, Q," said Emily. "And remember, we're going to practice the al— I mean, we're going to *read* together."

In the truck going home, Q thought that maybe he couldn't rely even on Emily to keep his secret. She was getting so much fun out of it, and he feared that the time might come when she'd simply have to share it with someone else, since for him it was far from being all fun. Should that happen, it would be all up with him in this town.

He sighed, and Mr. Wheatley said, "Something wrong, son?"

"No, boss." Not yet. "Could you tell me about your railroading days? I kind of fell asleep when you were talking this morning."

"Been overworking you, have I?"

Was it because it was Saturday? Because Mr. Wheatley was tired? Because he'd had a nice visit at the constable's house and been a big help to that family that he was now so unusually—*genial*? Q couldn't decide.

"When I was a boy, younger than you—" Mr. Wheatley began.

CHAPTER NINE

In the kitchen, in the big tin laundry tub, surrounded by screens, cozy and private, Q lathered his body and lifted his voice in song.

"*Oh, Shenandoah, I love your daughter! Way hey! you rolling river . . . 'tis seven long years since last I saw her . . . Way hey! we're bound away! 'Cross the wide Missooooori!*"

One afternoon, working outside the parlor windows with Mr. Wheatley, they had heard Augusta merrily tinkling on the piano keys, singing about the Shenandoah in a high sweet voice.

Q, listening, had got the words without trying. He'd found he could do this easily, and that once he'd conned words, he had them for good. Emily had told him what the various signs around town were, so that now, when he passed *Macky's Feed & Grain*, he knew what the red and gold sign signified. He knew that Dr. Anthony's shingle said *C. W. Anthony, M.D. Cartwright's Dairy* was lettered on the side of the horse-drawn wagon that pulled up to

Mrs. Benway's house each morning with milk and eggs and butter. There was *Forbes Dry Goods*, and the sign in the window said *Post Office*. All these, and more, were no longer mysterious to him. But he could not pretend that he was reading the letters and words. He'd been told what they were, and he remembered.

Emily assured him that with a memory like his the alphabet, and words themselves, were a hurdle he'd easily clear. He could hardly wait. Already he had a taste for books, grafted onto him by Emily's love for them.

Afternoons, when they were well beyond the bean-poles and the cornstalks, having picked their baskets full, she would take a book from the pocket of her pinafore and read to him for a short while. Fairy tales. Nursery Rhymes. *The Hollow Tree and Deep Woods Book*. *A Child's Garden of Verses*. He loved all of them. Every word. Every picture.

Except the tale of the *Emperor's New Clothes*. That put him in mind of himself, in reverse. The Emperor had paraded naked while the populace exclaimed at his beauti-ful clothes—because they'd been *told* he was wearing splendid new clothes, and after all, who would gainsay him? He was the Emperor. Until a little child in the crowd, caring nothing for crowns and the heads that wore them, piped up, "But he isn't wearing anything!" Q thought that that little child had probably looked like Andy Mears. Then all the people saw that indeed, indeed, their emperor didn't have a stitch on. *Would* little Andy Mears, who'd easily seen through the clothes Q wore (Q, who was no emperor), pipe up one day, "But look! He is a pig!" and everyone then see that indeed, indeed, this was not a runaway lad in their midst but a runaway boar?

———

He did not like that story and would not let it be read him again.

He liked to recite other stories to himself, other poems, too.

In Winter I get up at night
And dress by yellow candle-light.
In summer, quite the other way,
I have to go to bed by day.

That was nice. All the garden of verses was.

Now Tom would be a driver and Maria go to sea
And my papa's a banker and rich as he can be;
But I, when I am stronger and can choose what
*   I'm to do,*
Oh Leerie, I'll go round at night and light the
*   lamps with you!*

The town had gaslights now, but Emily said that when she was a very little girl there had still been a lamp-lighter who'd gone about in the evening to light the streetlamps and early in the morning to turn them off.

Always, now, Q had a sense of *learning*. From books. And from listening to people talk. There was Mrs. Benway's interesting kindly gossip. Emily's constant comment and speculation. Then there was Mr. Wheatley. Until today, his talk had consisted mostly of instructions, followed by, "Look alive, there, Q! Haven't got all day, you know," although, so far as Q could see, all day was just what they had.

But this afternoon, coming home in the truck, Mr. Wheatley had spoken in a husky voice of long-past days, when he had been a boy yearning to be a railroad man.

Henry Wheatley, nine years old, had left school and gone to work as a call-boy for the *Boston and Maine* that ran from Bangor to Boston to New York City. A call-boy with aspirations, who went through the town in the early dark hours of the morning rousing the railroad men so they'd get to the yard on time. A call-boy dreaming of one day becoming a fireman, or a conductor, or even an engineer (daring dreaming!) himself. At four o'clock every morning, in the rain, the snow, the soft summer dark, Henry Wheatley had trudged from house to house, awakening those powerful beings, the men of the *Boston and Maine*.

"But who woke you up?" Q had asked him.

"Me, myself, and I, son. My sense of duty woke me up. I have always had a strong sense of duty."

"But you didn't become a railroad man?"

Mr. Wheatley snorted and pushed his jaw forward. "I got blackballed by the powers-that-be, Q."

"Why?"

"You can ask. Well— I'll tell you why. As an object lesson for you to learn by, seeing as how I have sort of sponsored you and feel responsible for how you behave. Isn't the sort of fairy tale I tell the Mears youngsters."

Q, who'd listened half-awake to about half the morning's railroad adventures, said, "You told them you were an engineer."

"That's just a *story* I tell to entertain the imps. They want to hear about important stuff, engi*nee*ring stuff, so that's what I tell them. Can't hurt. If they never hear worse lies— Well, let it go. I'll tell *you* the facts, Q, and you profit

by them, hear? Then maybe some good will come of—
All right, here's the whole sad story. I was a call-boy till I
got to be around fourteen. Then I was put to walking ties,
checking switches, with an older guy showing me the
ropes. Big bad-tempered slob. Never gave me a word of
encouragement. Bad-mouthed me to the higher-ups. Well,
him and me got in a fight over something, hanged if I've
ever been able to remember what it was. Anyway, I beat
the tar out of him. I wasn't always the easygoing fellow
I am now," he said, and Q's eyes widened. "I was a burly
son-of-a-gun, and I laid him right out. I *was* going to leave
him on the tracks for the six-thirty to run over him, but
I reconsidered."

Q looked sideways at his boss, to see if he was making
an awful joke. No. Mr. Wheatley's face showed that he was
seriously telling a true story. "I figured," Mr. Wheatley went
on, "that that would get me in even worse trouble than I
was already going to be in."

"I guess so," murmured Q.

"But nobody listened to my side at all. Blackballed me
clear across the country. Time they were through, I couldn't
have got a job sweeping up cigar butts on a trunk line from
Podunk to Dopunk. I never had a *chance*, that's how they
fixed it. Still, I've made my way. I haven't done so bad.
And let me tell you one thing, Quentin Corn, I worked on
that terrible temper of mine till I subdued it, and I advise
you to do likewise."

"I don't have a temper," Q said. "I don't think I have."

"You can't tell about a temper. That's the reason I'm
letting you in on all this, so's you can profit by how bad I

was treated. A temper's like a snake. Can be coiled up, quiet as can be, and first thing you know—*wham* and you're bit."

Q didn't think this was so, but felt reluctant to argue with a man who'd leave another man on the railroad track for the 6:13 to run over. Even if he'd reconsidered. It had all been a lot of years ago, but Mr. Wheatley was still sore as a boil, and if his temper was a snake, Q was not the lad, or pig, to prod it awake.

Anyway, he thought now, lathering his back, that explains why he's so grouchy most of the time. Except with the Mears family and Mrs. Benway. He supposed that everybody had to have somebody to be nice to.

"*O, Shenandoah, I long to see you! Way hey, you rooollling river! . . .*"

Mrs. Benway had given him some work-clothes left behind by Pete. He got out of the tub, toweled himself, took the shirt and pants from the top of the screen, and tugged them on. Pete, when he left home, must've been a little smaller than Q. Upstairs, in his room that had been Pete's room, a Sunday go-to-church outfit was arranged on a ladderback chair. He was uneasy about going to church tomorrow, but there seemed no way to avoid it. Mrs. Benway just assumed he'd be going with her and Mr. Scott. Maybe he could pretend to be sick? He shook his head. Except for his huge, his *enormous* lie, and the little lies that had to surround it protectively, he'd found himself to be a truthful person now that he was a person. Well, he could not truthfully claim to be truthful while carrying on this deception, but he did avoid lies when he could.

So, there was no ducking it. He'd have to go to church and there be, for the first time since he'd arrived, squarely in the town's eye. That might be the end of Quentin Corn, strong young fellow with not much brain who had run away from an orphanage and was now trying to make his way in the world. One thing, he was going to sit at the back of the church, near the door, ready to run if discovered.

Meanwhile, the bath and the clean clothes had made him feel fine. He was, like any pig, happy to be clean if given the chance.

He put the screens away in a room called the summer kitchen where Mrs. Benway did her ironing and put up fruits and vegetables and preserves from her garden. He dipped a basin in the washtub and emptied the bathwater out the back door until the tub was light enough to hoist and carry into the yard, where he rinsed it at the pump and left it, as he'd been told, to air. All the while, he was singing.

"*I'm lonesome since I crossed the hill and o'er the moor and vaaalley! Such lonesome thoughts my heart do fill, since parting with my Saally!*"

Mrs. Benway was sitting on the porch swing, fanning herself, creaking back and forth. She looked up when Q came out, and said, "I declare, Quentin, you have the sweetest voice. I was saying to Mr. Scott, 'fore he left, I don't recall a voice quite like it. A true boy's soprano but with a sort of—you know, it's funny, I said to Mr. Scott, but it almost sounds like sort of a *squeal*."

There goes singing, thought Q. I sure better not sing anymore.

"If," Mrs. Benway was going on, "a squeal can be musical, then you have a musical squeal in your voice." She laughed heartily as Q slumped on the steps where Mr. Scott usually sat. "You are going to have to try out for Choir," said Mrs. Benway.

"Oh, no!" Q exclaimed. "I couldn't do that!"

"Pshaw. Acourse you can, and you're going to."

"Mrs. Benway! Please, please. I'm too shy. I'm terribly shy. I'd get a rash. I'd choke. I'd faint."

"Stuff and nonsense," she said, calmly creaking back and forth. "We need a voice like yours. Never did hear the like before. No, I'm going to take you right up to Mr. Carberry, he's our choirmaster, after services tomorrow, and when he hears *you*! Why, the man's going to be happier than a robin in a compost heap."

"But I don't think—"

"No need of that, ha-ha. Person with a voice like yours—no need to bother thinking." She frowned faintly. "Pity you're probably just about ready to lose it."

"Lose what?" Q asked despondently.

"Your voice, Quentin. Your voice, acourse. You are probably just about ready for your voice change. I warrant we won't get more'n one season out of you for Choir."

Entirely cast down at what had come of just feeling happy in the washtub, Q did not reply.

After a while, Mrs. Benway said, "Those duds are a mite small on you. I'll have to let them out at the seams. You find your church outfit all right?"

Q nodded.

"Good. Well, what about a game of Parcheesi?"

CHAPTER TEN

Summoning bells in the steeple rang. The gold hands of the steeple clock positioned themselves at ix and dropped nine deep notes under the bells' high pealing.

Q and Mrs. Benway entered the church with the last comers, he miserable, she fretful. She had tried repeatedly to hurry him since breakfast, and Q had made repeated efforts to delay. But here they were, inside, no going back.

"Down the aisle here," she said in an exasperated whisper. "We'll sit next to Mr. and Mrs. Cartwright. Come *along*, Quentin."

Quentin, to his relief, saw Mr. Wheatley and the Mears clan sitting in the last pew. "You go," he whispered back. "I'll sit there with Mr. Wheatley."

She clucked, but hastened away, and Q slipped into the aisle seat, next to his boss, who nodded at him approvingly. For being here? For being dressed in Pete's best? Q had been uncomfortable about meeting Mr. Wheatley again, after that terrible story, but the big man seemed as usual, except tidier and with a peaceful expression Q hadn't observed on him before.

At a small organ an elderly man was playing. Q thought the music sounded fine and happy. Hearing it, he even managed to relax.

The church was full of dressed-for-Sunday worshipers. The Mears girls, in fresh flour sacks with ribbons in their yellow hair, were arrayed for church like flowers. Andy, sitting on the other side of Mr. Wheatley, had plainly had his umbrella outfit washed and pressed, his bright hair slicked down. Mrs. Mears, in a print dress and a small blue straw hat, sat with her hands in her lap, eyes cast down. All her girls, ranged to one side of her, sat with eyes cast down, hands in lap. Andy peered around Mr. Wheatley's stomach and fixed his serene gaze on Q, who decided Emily was right. Andy looked as if he liked having a secret and would like keeping it.

It was hot. All the windows were open. Through one of them Q saw Constable Mears pedal by. Mr. Wheatley said that the constable was never really off duty but took time to go to evening services on Sunday. Most human beings, thought Q, lead harder lives than pigs do. But Constable Mears always looked contented. Probably because he had a nice wife and a pretty litter.

To Q's relief, the big doors at the back were also left open. At the first sign of discovery, at the first even doubtful *look*, he was going to scram out of here. He had the whole scene in his mind. Someone turns—as Emily now was squirming around in a pew way down front to catch his eye and smile—someone *not* Emily turns and casually glances at him, looks away, looks back puzzled, frowns and looks away again, then back, and says, poking his neighbor, "Am I crazy or—no, no, I gotta be crazy—but look, *you* look and tell me—*is* that, *can* that be—will you just *look* back there and tell me I shouldn't have drunk that extra glass of applejack last night . . ." That, or something like it. He was going to be alert every second of this service, ready to beat it—

Because if that suspicious glance once settled on him and came to a conclusion—the right one—he'd have no choice. Leaving this town, he would miss Emily. Miss her a lot. He'd miss Mrs. Benway and even, in a funny way, Mr. Wheatley. But he did not think, not for one instant, that Mrs. Benway and Mr. Wheatley would see the matter as Emily did. "A PIG! He's been sleeping in my son's bed and wearing my son's clothes and *bathing in my washtub!*" "A pig! I been telling my life's story *to a pig!* Trying to help a pig make a better life for himself? And paying him three bucks a week! My trouble is I'm too easygoing . . . a PIG!"

That was how Mrs. Benway and Mr. Wheatley would take the unveiling of the runaway boy they'd been so kind to. They would say he'd deceived them. Of course, he had. That it had been a choice for him between masquerading as a boy or being barbecued as a pig would not signify. They'd figure that as a pig it was his duty to be barbecued. Mr. Wheatley, especially, was keen on duty. Q thought that probably Mrs. Benway, after he was actually cooked, would be too sentimental to eat him. "No, no . . . I just couldn't keep him down. In spite of everything, I *liked* him. And he did have *such* a pretty voice, with that musical squeal in it . . ." But Mr. Wheatley! *Well.* "Darned if the youngster don't taste pretty good at that . . ."

That was how, as Quentin Corn saw it, his landlady and his boss would react if his pigness were brought to light. That every passing day made him feel less like a boar and more like a boy would not, he feared, tip the balance with people who relished their pork pies and bacon the way human beings did.

Thus reflecting, he did not observe the members of the choir as they filed in, took their positions, and opened their books. It was when their voices rang out that he forgot himself, forgot everything and everyone around him. He heard only their singing.

He liked to hear Augusta at the piano, to hear Augusta's singing. Since his piglethood he had enjoyed the songs of birds. And he liked his own singing very well. But this chorus of men's and women's and boys' voices was like no sound he had ever heard before. Emily had told him about heaven, and about how all the people and animals were going to go there after they died. "Except," she'd said, "a few *very* bad people." She'd thought for a moment and added, "I don't think there are any bad animals." "I don't know about that," said Q. "There was a dog at Qui—" He'd broken off. Not even to Emily had he confided what farm he'd run from. "—At the place where I was. He had a temper like the edge of an axe." "Oh, Q—you don't go to hell for having a bad temper. You go for being *wicked.*" "Well, he had a wicked temper." Emily had just laughed and said that since he'd never encountered wickedness he didn't know what it was. "Have you?" he asked. "No," she answered him seriously. "Not yet, anyway."

But, thought Q—to whom all this had occurred so fleetingly that he was almost unaware of having thought it—but this sound, this singing, must be what people and animals went to heaven for. There they were, townspeople transformed by beautiful blue robes with white collars, holding their books before them and singing, thought Q, like the angels Emily says they are going to meet when they leave this world and go to the next.

> Listen to the lambs . . . all acrying!
> Listen to the lambs . . . all accrrying!
> He shall feed his flock like a shepherd
> And carry . . . the young lambs . . . in his bosom!

As Q listened to the choir, he was all acrying. At least, tears—the first he'd ever known—welled in his eyes as the music of their voices gladdened his ears and entranced his spirit. They sang of the shepherd carrying the young lambs in his bosom, and to Q it was a picture, a sound, so beautiful that tears fell from his eyes and plopped on Pete's Sunday pants.

> I bless Thee, Lord, because I grow
> Among Thy trees, which in a row
> To Thee both fruit and order owe.
> What open force, or hidden charm
> Can blast my fruit, or bring me harm,
> While the inclosure is Thine arm . . .

When Reverend Emerson climbed the short flight of winding stairs to his pulpit, Q took no notice. The choir members were seated now, and the congregation lifted its head attentively as Mr. Emerson said, "The lesson for to-day—" Q heard him not, nor did he notice whether anyone was noticing him. Such matters were forgotten, lost in the songs that still echoed in his mind. He sat unheeding through the service until, at the last, the choir rose again.

> *Rock of ages, cleft for me,*
> *Let me hide myself in thee . . .*

When Emily had talked of heaven he had not, in truth, quite believed her. Not for himself, in any case. It sounded far too glorious to be something awaiting a humble pig. Probably, he'd decided, she was wrong about animals going there. Maybe birds, who sang so prettily and already had wings. But a plain old porker? He didn't think so.

Now he made his mind up. He was going. If there was this kind of singing in the choir stall of a little country church, what was going on, right this *moment*, in heaven, in the way of music?

And Mrs. Benway wanted *him*, Quentin Corn, former pig, to sing with *them*, that choir of townspeople in their robes, divinely touched with song on Sunday morning? She's loopy, thought Q, and the minute the services were over he scooted out the door, around the church, across the churchyard, past the rectory, down the lanes of pole beans and cornstalks and tomatoes to the place under the elm tree where sometimes Emily read to him.

He lay there on the grass, panting.

He would have to go back to the boardinghouse this morning, of course. But he was going to wait until all chance of the choirmaster and Mrs. Benway's catching him was past. Maybe, if he got there when Mrs. Benway was busy with noonday dinner, and maybe if all next week he never sang a note, she'd forget that she'd had such a—such a *loopy* notion.

"Q!" Emily's voice, somewhere in the cornstalks. "Q! I know you're there!"

He thought he wouldn't answer. But resisting Emily's call was more than he could do, so he stood and waved.

"I knew it," she said. "I guessed you'd come here. Why did you run away?"

"Shhh! Don't talk so loud. I'm hiding."

"Why?"

"Mrs. Benway said she was going to make me meet the choirmaster and try out for the choir."

"Well, that's right, and she should, if you have a voice like she says. She says you have a simply lovely soprano and we *need* a good boy's voice, and how could you *do* this, Q?"

Q's spirits sagged. He flung himself on the ground and groaned. "Everybody's crazy." He sat up. "Emily—I can't sing with those—those—" He could not express what he felt about this choir, which he was sure would be re-formed as soon as all the members got to heaven.

"They aren't the best singing group in the world, but my gosh, Q, what do you expect in a little town like this? If you'd agree to sing and they *had* a good soprano, maybe things would improve."

"Im*prove*! Emily, they are the most beautiful, the most wonderful, the most—most *heavenly* choir I ever heard!"

"How many is that?"

Q scowled. "That's not fair. They didn't take me to *church* at Qui—at the farm. They weren't interested in my *soul*. They were interested in my *ribs*."

"Oh, stop it, Q. You're always talking about that and I say you should stop thinking about it, and stop talking about it, because stopping talking about it is the beginning of stopping thinking about it. *You are not a pig.* You are my friend, and Mr. Wheatley's helper, and Mrs. Benway's boarder. You are a boy named Quentin Corn."

Q straightened. She was right. He did tend to dwell too much on his past as pig and not enough on his present as person. The difficulty being that he didn't feel like a pig *or* a person. He no longer knew what he was. Emily was the only clear and certain presence in his foggy straits. And now here she was, trying to put him in the awful position of daring to join the *choir*! Pretending that it wasn't even a good choir, so as to lull him into agreement.

Not to his surprise, he got lulled. He trudged after her back through the tomatoes, the cornstalks, the pole beans, past the rectory, through the churchyard, and so to the side church door and in.

With Mrs. Benway, all smiles, stood Mr. Carberry, organist and choirmaster. "Well, well, well," he said with an encouraging laugh. "So this is Quentin. We thought you'd run away from us."

Q smiled weakly. Then, with resolution, said, "I did run away. I can't . . . I'm not *good* enough to sing in your choir."

"Stuff and nonsense, Quentin," said Mrs. Benway. "Let us be the judge of that."

Mr. Carberry handed Q a hymnal and said, "Suppose

you try, ah—let's see—number one-sixty-four. *In the Garden.*"

Q cast a look of anguish at Emily. He hadn't even got to the alphabet yet. How was he supposed to read a hymn?

"I know what," Emily said brightly. "I'll bet Q—I mean, Quentin—knows one of the hymns that was sung this morning. Don't you, Q? Quentin."

"I know them all," he said, and of course he did, having heard them and listened with complete attention.

"Excellent, excellent," said Mr. Carberry. "I'll just give you an A here, Quentin, and then you lift up your voice unto the Lord. *A capella.*"

"*A capella?*"

"Unaccompanied," said Mrs. Benway. "No organ. Just you, singing."

Q swallowed nervously and shook his head. "I can't. That's all. I just can't."

"Oh, my. The lad's timid," said Mr. Carberry. Like everyone except Emily and Andy, he took Q for what he was dressed as, what he was said to be. In this case, a boy with a fine soprano who could definitely be used by the choir.

"I have an idea," said Emily. "Let's put a robe on him. Then he'd get more of a feeling for the part."

"Oh, capital idea," said Mr. Carberry, and Mrs. Benway nodded and said, "That might do it."

Doomed but resigned, Q followed Emily into a small room behind the organ. Against the wall was a rack of blue robes with white collars, all sizes. Emily selected one, held it against him, and said, "There. That should fit. Let's get it on you."

Q, dazzled at the thought, lifted his arms and let her slide the garment over his head. Then, in a dreamy way, moved by the touch of her prodding finger, he looked at himself in the mirror.

"But I'm beautiful," he whispered, gazing at the reflection of a choirboy that was his very own self. "Just beautiful."

"Of course you are. And you have a beautiful voice and you're going to *sing* with it."

Feeling like Cinderella, transformed by clothes, Q said, "Of course I am," and marched out to Mr. Carberry.

Q sang *Listen to the Lambs*, and *Rock of Ages*, and brought tears to Mr. Carberry's eyes and to Emily's and to Mrs. Benway's. Also to his own.

"Now then, Quentin," said Mr. Carberry, "you will come to choir practice Wednesday and Friday evenings." He sounded very excited. "Don't do anything foolish like catching cold or breaking your leg, and—oh, my word, is this not marvelous? Mrs. Benway, how can I thank you? And Emily. And, of course, Quentin Corn—how can I thank *you* enough for coming among us with your heaven-sent voice?"

Q, dazed by praise, dumbstruck at finding he could sing at all, much less as well as they seemed to think, confounded at everything that had happened to him since waking in his sty six days ago, was robbed of speech. He surrendered his robe to Emily and waited mutely for whatever came next.

"All right, young fellow," said Mrs. Benway. "Back to earth. We must go right home. You have chores to do, and I must see to the roast. There's a nice chicken salad for you," she added hastily, as Q's eyes tended to roll at the sound of words like "roast."

"Mrs. Benway," said Emily, "I was—I mean, we were —hoping Q could have Sunday dinner with us. Mama says yes and we'd like it awfully."

"That's very kind of your mother," Mrs. Benway said doubtfully. "But Quentin does have his chores to do . . . Oh well, I won't say no. But Quentin, hurry home right after dinner, mind. Quentin! Say thank you to Emily, like a good lad."

But Quentin only blinked at her and did not say a word.

"He's overcome," Mr. Carberry said compassionately. As Q left with Emily, he heard the choirmaster add, "You certainly are right, Mrs. Benway. There *is* a sort of melodic squeal in that voice. *Most* unusual."

Q shivered, as if removing the robe had exposed him to cold reality on this hot summer day.

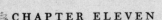

CHAPTER ELEVEN

o far, Quentin Corn had been in two houses. There was Mrs. Benway's with its trim front and back yards, its birdbath surrounded by geraniums and petunias, its stand of sunflowers screening the privy out back. In Mrs. Benway's house the floors were bare with handmade rag rugs and polished boards. The windows sparkled, the wallpapers and furniture-covers were faded and immaculate. Then there had been the Mears cottage with its shabby front yard, its small dark rooms, narrow hallway, its air of neglect past redeeming, no matter how Mr. Wheatley tried.

Q had thought Mrs. Benway's house grand past imagining, until today when he walked with Emily into the rectory parlor. It would have taken his breath away if he'd been able to catch it yet.

Trying to see it all at once, he managed a dazzled impression of color. A big blue carpet with flowers woven into it, red velvet chairs and a long green sofa, fluffy cushions and china trinkets, a brass coal-scuttle, lamps with ruby bases and white china shades, large bowls of flowers. Two tall windows flanked the fireplace, and there were even flowers there, in the hearth. There was a high-backed chair done entirely in needlework, flowery too. Against the wall was Augusta's piano, darkly gleaming, with a panel of gathered pink silk in the center and a lacy music rack. Near the open windows at the far side of the room was a round table, draped with a rose velvet shawl with deep fringe around it. In the center of the table, on the shawl, was a blue glass vase with crystal drops.

Q found his voice. "I didn't know you lived in a *palace*, Emily." She had read to him about palaces, in the fairy tales, and now here he was—in one.

But Emily laughed. "Oh, Q, it isn't a palace. It's just a very nice house that goes with the church, and we don't even own it, the parish does."

Knowing no palace could be grander, Q stood rooted in the doorway. He didn't see how anyone could ever *use* such a room, actually walk into it and sit on the velvet chairs—they had fringe, too, and tassels. He didn't see how anyone could go in and sit down and look at everything.

"Come *on*, Q," said Emily. When he didn't move, she put her hands against his back and shoved. "You aren't going to wear anything *out*, you know."

That was just what Q had been thinking he would do. It seemed to him that a steady gaze would shatter the blue vase, wilt the flowers, wear out the velvet, send the piano keys tinkling to the floor.

"I think I'll go back to Mrs. Benway's," he said. "A pig doesn't belong here."

"Now you really make me angry, Q. What you are saying, of course, is that Mrs. Benway's nice house is good enough for a pig, but this place isn't, and even if you didn't mean to say it, which I guess you didn't, it is *not nice . . .*"

Before he could defend himself, Augusta came in. "What's *not nice*. Emily?" she demanded. "Are you bullying your guest already? Don't mind her, Quentin. She tries to intimidate everybody, but we all resist her. Don't we, little sister?" she said affectionately.

"I don't bully. I just have a candid nature, so I try to point out people's mistakes. To help them. I'm helping Q to improve himself."

"I can't see that he requires improvement, but he seems willing to put up with you, so that's his affair. But kindly make no effort, Emily, to improve Mr. Scott, who is coming for dinner." She turned to Q. "Mama tells me we're to have the pleasure of your company, too, Quentin."

He bobbed his head wordlessly, and then, with desperation, not wanting to be considered a dumb *oaf*, he said, "I like to hear you when you play the piano, ma'am."

"Ma'am, is it? You make me feel like an old lady."

Q gulped and looked at her helplessly. She patted him on the head and said, "That's all right. I'm afraid we're all teases in this house, and you must take us as you find us. Call me Augusta. If you can't manage that, Miss Emerson. Ma'am is for Mama."

"Now who's bullying?" said Emily.

"Is somebody?" Sophy asked, sailing into the room as if blown there. "Bullying? For shame. I think it's going to rain. Josephine has come out of the barn."

They all laughed, and Sophy said to Q, "You see, we have this *odd* horse. Papa's buggy bay. That is, the bay that pulls Papa's buggy . . . yes, that sounds better. Her name is Josephine, and she only likes in*clement* weather. If it snows or rains or sleets, she stands out in her corral, and when the sun shines she goes back in the barn. Everyone in this family is peculiar," she said proudly.

"Is Josephine part of the family?" Q asked curiously.

"Of course she is," said Sophy, and Augusta said, "Quentin likes to hear me play, so I shall play until Mr. Scott arrives."

"So he can hear you as he arrives," said Sophy.

"Sit down, all," said Augusta. "I shall render *Humoresque*."

Q, now well into the room, started to sink to the edge of the needlework chair.

"Not there!" Sophy cried, and he shot up shaking. "Oh dear," she said, "I didn't mean to alarm you. No, but that's my petit-point masterpiece and I never let anyone, not even Papa, sit on it."

"It's to be handed down from generation to generation, even unto the seventh, unsat-upon," said Augusta.

"It's awfully pretty," said Q, looking for a place where it might be safe to perch.

"Oh, come here, Q," said Emily. "Sit with me on the sofa. We don't plan for *it* to go further than Augusta's great-grandchildren."

"Emily, don't say daring things. It doesn't become you," said Augusta, twirling the piano stool. "Now, first *Humoresque*, and after that—"

But then Mr. and Mrs. Emerson entered with Mr. Scott, and when greetings had been exchanged they moved into the dining room.

"Quentin," said Mrs. Emerson, when grace was over, "Emily tells me that you are a vegetarian—"

"Goodness," said Sophy. "I don't think I—"

She was frowned into silence by her mother, who continued, "So we have a special platter for you. And now, Mr. Emerson, if you will carve the Sunday ham?"

Stepping to the sideboard, Mr. Emerson took up a long shining knife, moved it back and forth with graceful motions along a tapering sharpener, and addressed himself to the Sunday ham.

Q, with a deep steadying breath, looked at Emily. She lifted her shoulders a little. Not my fault, she said without words. And of course it was not, but to Q's sensitive mind, she seemed a little bored, and he wished he had gone back to his chicken salad and his chores.

Augusta and Sophy, both members of the choir, said they could hardly wait for Wednesday evening practice, in order to hear Q, and Mrs. Emerson, sensing his discomfort, turned to Mr. Scott with questions about his plans for the coming school year, and from that they went on to discuss Mr. Emerson's sermon, Sophy saying that she *thought* her father had made a grammatical error.

"Impossible," said Mrs. Emerson.

"Barely possible," said her husband.

Conversation flourished, though Emily contributed little. It was a nice, interesting, kind, lively family, and Q wished he felt more comfortable with them.

During dinner there was a distant sound of thunder

tumbling in the hills, mingled with the plaintive far-off cry of the *Boston and Maine*, traveling to Bangor. But the sun continued to shine through the windows upon glittering glasses, pure white linen, a bowl of sweet peas, shining silver, and plates of Sunday ham with sweet potatoes and beans.

For seven days now, Q had been eating at table with human beings, handling his knife and fork with ease, showing off his nice table manners. He was thinking that this was quite the longest meal—

There was a crash from the parlor.

"What the deuce is that?" said the Reverend Wendell Emerson, jumping from his chair and rushing from the room, followed by family and guests.

"Hey!" he shouted. "Hey, hey, hey! Stop that! Josephine, stop that right now!"

Big head shoved through the open window, Josephine was nibbling at the rose velvet shawl on the table. Fringes dripped to either side of her mouth in long silk mustaches, and she gazed at the group in the parlor while she chewed and drew the shawl toward her like an enormous bib. The blue glass vase with crystal drops lay in shards on the floor.

Mr. Emerson bounded across the room, seized the other end of the shawl, and began a tug of war with his buggy bay while Mrs. Emerson waved her fists in anger.

"She's not only eating my beautiful Spanish shawl, she is *standing* in the border! My flowers will be ruined!"

All the shouting disconcerted Josephine, who gave a sharp look at those in the room, whinnied, and dropped her side of the shawl. She raced back to her corral, throw-

ing up clods of dirt and grass as she crossed the thick, once-tidy lawn.

Mrs. Emerson, picking up the wet, chewed, grass-stained shawl, looked at it sadly. "I must tell myself that it was only a *thing*. A material thing. I must remind myself that material things are not important—"

"Who left that corral gate open?" Mr. Emerson demanded. He did not appear to expect a confession, and there was none.

"Do you *know*," said Augusta, "that horse whinnied at us in a most defiant manner. I don't think she's the least *bit* repentant."

Sophy, taking the shawl from her mother, said, "I'll just cut away the insulted portion, and the rest I can use in my quilt. My goodness, Mama, just think how pretty this will be, along with that creamy moire you gave me. It'll be quite the most elegant quilt anyone ever—"

"I am going to my room to swoon briefly," said Mrs. Emerson. "Mr. Scott, Quentin, I am sure you will excuse me." She went, the back of her hand to her mouth in a vexed, unhappy gesture.

"Well," said Augusta. "I suppose we could go in and have dessert."

Q pulled Emily aside. "I am going back and do my chores. I have an awful lot of—"

"All right, Q. We *were* going to play croquet afterwards. The dessert is cherry pie. Are you sure— Actually, I'm not very hungry—"

"I'll go," he said nervously. "Tell everybody thank you for me."

"All right . . . if you must. It's been pretty hectic. Anyway," she added, as the room darkened and thunder threatened closer, "probably we won't be able to play. Josephine was right. It's going to rain." She glanced down at the broken vase. "Probably I should clean that up," she said listlessly.

"Could I—"

"Oh, no. But thank you," she said, and seemed, for the first time since they'd met, to have lost her consuming interest in Quentin Corn.

Running home, hoping to get there before Pete's garments were rained on, Q thought sadly that he was beginning to wear out his welcome. He did not blame Emily. How long could he expect a little human girl to go on enjoying the companionship of a pig? But if she did get tired of him, would she make a slip—not meaning to at all, but just because his secret was no longer so important to her—and say something that would reveal his true identity to the entire town?

And then there was Josephine.

When the horse had looked into the roomful of people —of supposed people—she had fixed her eye on him, and that whinny that Augusta had thought defiant was actually a simple question directed at Q.

"What in the name of oats do you think *you're* doing in there?" she'd whinnied, and Q, in spite of all he treasured about his present life, had felt tugged away from that palace room, that family, the memory of himself in choir robes singing unto the Lord. Tugged away from Emily, whom he loved. He had felt a stab of yearning for that other world, the animal one he had been born to and belonged in, no matter what its perils.

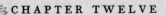

CHAPTER TWELVE

As Q reached Mrs. Benway's front porch the clouds that had been piling in great dark domes over the town let spill their burden. In minutes gutters and drains rushed with water, geraniums and petunias were flattened to earth, the birdbath brimmed and spilled over.

"Oh my goodness, Quentin. There you are! What a blessing. Help me get the house closed . . . you do upstairs, I'll do down!"

Q flew up the staircase and ran from room to room hurling down windows, though the rain, driving heavily from the west, had already drenched the floor beneath his window and that in Mr. Scott's room. On the east side, where Mrs. Benway's bedroom was, and the sewing room, things were still dry.

He got towels to mop up the floors, then removed Pete's Sunday suit and got into his own old garments, the pants and shirt and bandanna he had taken from the clothesline at Farmer Quigley's that fateful morning.

Downstairs, he found Mrs. Benway leaning back in an old rocker in the summer kitchen, also east-facing. He sat beside her in the other chair and for a while they gazed contentedly at the streaking rain. There was a wild peppery scent on the air. Thunder crashed and lightning sped out of the sky in brilliant stripes. The trees swayed, branches thrashing. Sunflowers tugged at their stakes, bending huge sodden heads. From a downspout at the corner of the house water splashed into a rain barrel. And again the lonely whistle blew . . . the *Boston and Maine*, going south this time, having passed its sister going north. Long after it had passed the town, they could hear that wavering cry streaming behind it in the storm.

"Isn't it wonderful, Quentin?" said Mrs. Benway. "I began to think we'd turn into a dustbowl. Reminds me of that song . . . dee, dee, dee . . . how does it go? Something about a flower—*lying there sighing for one drop of rain.* Dah, dah, dah . . . and love and sorrow and so forth. Very sweet song. I don't recall it exactly. But I must tell you how proud I am of you. And Mr. Carberry! 'Why,' he said to me, 'Mrs. Benway, if it only lasts through Christmas'—your voice, before it breaks—'if it only lasts through Christmas,' he said, 'my joy will be unconfined.'"

Q squirmed under her praise, saying nothing.

"Modest," she said placidly. "Helpful and modest." She sighed. Remembering Pete? Q wondered. Her son, who had been neither, according to Mr. Wheatley. Pete Benway, Emily had told him, had helped himself to all the money his mother had in the house before skedaddling no one knew where. "Nobody knows how much she had, Q. Fact is, Mrs. Benway's never said a word about it to anyone. It was that drummer, Mr. Hargraves, who boards with her. He told what Pete had done, though he shouldn't have. And he didn't even leave a note on the pincushion. Pete, I mean."

"Pincushion?" Q said.

"It's an *expression*, Q. If somebody—well, say a girl *elopes*. Well, she's supposed to leave a note for her family saying how sorry she is on the pincushion. I suppose so it won't blow off? What I mean is, Pete Benway took his mother's money and just went without a word. Awful. Just awful."

But Mrs. Benway didn't seem sad now. Just quiet and contented, rocking in her rocker, watching the rain.

"It smells good," Q said. "The rain."

"It surely does. Thought we'd never see it again," she said, and all at once gave a low gasp, braced her feet to stop the rocker, and said in a low voice, "Upstairs, Q! Run! Quickly!"

"But—"

"Do as I say! Right *now!*"

Confused enough to be frightened, Q ran. He scooted out of the summer kitchen, through the kitchen, across the front room, and up the stairs to his own room.

What was happening? Why had he had to run? What was it *about*? Standing perplexed and anxious in his doorway, he turned suddenly and tiptoed into Mrs. Benway's bedroom and peered out of the window into the back yard, where Mrs. Benway had been looking when she jammed her feet down and said *"Run!"* What had she *seen* there?

Crouched at the sill, he looked through the driving

rain. Was someone walking there? Yes, he could discern a figure approaching the house, sauntering in sodden clothes as if the sun were shining.

Could it be Mr. Hargraves, back from traveling in ladies' corsets? Coming through the back yard, without a suitcase, swaggering through the dark and the rain like that?

No, not Mr. Hargraves.

Q knew who it was. Pete Benway. No one else it could be. Realizing this, he felt his heart drop, his knees wobble. This was trouble. He didn't know what kind, and he didn't know how much, but Pete Benway was going to spell trouble for Quentin Corn.

He started across the hall to return to his room, but stopped when he heard voices from downstairs. Carefully, step by step, he descended until he was able to hear them as they spoke in the kitchen.

"I tell you, I want something to eat first, Ma. Cut out the questions, and the nagging about wet clothes. I'm starved."

"You're soaking wet."

"Worried about me, or the furniture?"

"The furniture," she said stiffly.

"Nice talk from a fellow's mother. What've you got to eat around here?"

"Pot roast. It's cold."

"I don't care. Give me some. Any of your bread? Can't begin to tell you how many times I've thought about your bread."

"I wouldn't have thought you'd think about anything about your home."

"Now, now, Ma. Keep yer apron on. Young fellows leave home all the time, you know that."

"They don't all rob their mothers as they go."

"What was I supposed to travel on, my good looks? Hadda have a stake, didn't I? Suppose I'd asked for the money, what then?"

"I might've said yes and I might've said no, but you should have asked."

"I sure thought I'd get a better welcome than this."

Silence from Mrs. Benway. Slurping sounds from Pete. Then, after a while, "Piece of that cake, Ma."

"You might say please."

"So . . . please."

Another silence, then the grating of a chair as Pete got up. "*Now* I'll go to my room and change."

"Oh, but—but you can't! I'll get your—some clothes for you. You wait here—"

"What d'ya mean, wait here? I'm going up to my room and change into dry clothes. I'm soaked right through."

"Pete, wait! It isn't your room. Not anymore."

"And what is that supposed to mean? *Exactly*."

"It means that I have to—to contrive to get along. And how I do it is taking in boarders, which you very well know. And your room is occupied. By a very nice young man. Boy."

"Aha! Got yourself a substitute son, have you?"

"It isn't that at all. You've been gone for two years. The room was empty and this nice lad, works for Mr. Wheatley, took it, and—"

"That old duffer still hanging around?"

"He is not an—I won't listen to this."

"I don't care what you listen to, Ma. Just get the nice lad works for Mr. Wheatley outa my room. No, don't bother. I'll do it myself."

"Ohhh!" Mrs. Benway's cry was from the heart. "Pete, why did you come back? You've been nothing but grief to me, ever. I was used to having you gone, I'd got over my heartache—"

"Heartache! Heartache my left hind footache, Ma. You were *glad* to have me gone."

"Maybe I was, maybe I was. But that didn't stop the heartache. You're my son," she said with a soft sob. "A mother can't forget her son, or not ache for him, no matter what."

"You seem to have made a good start. Well, enough of the gab. This nice young lad works for old duffer Wheatley at home now, or do I have to wait till he gets here to throw him out?"

"You are *not* going to throw him out! I won't let you!" Mrs. Benway sounded all at once firm.

"Ma, get outa my way."

"I won't!"

"Now, look"—sounding patient—"look, I could fold you up and store you in the pantry, but I don't want to hafta. Like you say, you're my mother. But you better get out of the way or you'll find yourself trussed up with the pickles and potatoes."

Sound of footsteps stamping from the kitchen.

Q fled up the stairs and ran, without thinking, to his room. *Pete's* room. Once there, he realized that he was trapped. He glanced wildly about for a place to hide. Under the bed? And what then? How long before he had to come out and face—whatever he had to face?

Better to do it now. Brazen it out. And he could always, he supposed, find another boardinghouse. Not that another could ever be like—

The door flew open and there was Pete Benway, small eyes widening in astonishment.

"What the—holy smoke! A dressed-up *pig* in my room. What's the old lady think she's doing?" He scratched his head, turned toward the hall, turned back, gaping. "I gotta wake up . . . I'm asleep, that's it. Because I *think* I am seeing a pig in my bedroom, and that's just gotta be a dream."

So, thought Q. Another one. Emily, Andy, now Pete. All had seen through his disguise without a moment's doubt. (He did not count Josephine, since of course a horse would know a pig when she saw one. His safety from her had been in the fact that she couldn't whinny the truth abroad.)

But what did Emily, Andy, and Pete Benway have in common? They were all young and clever. Was that enough? Yes, it had proved to be enough. But he did not think that Pete, like Emily and Andy for their different reasons, would *keep* his secret. This one would whoop it all over town.

Pete advanced warily into the room, put out a cautious finger, and touched Q, who was sitting upright in a chair, on the nose.

"By gum," he said. "You're really there. You're a pig, sitting in my chair, in my room, all dressed up in regular clothes. I mean, you're not some crazy thing I'm making up in my head . . ."

"No," said Q.

Pete jumped back. "Holy mother! It talks!"

"Courage, Q. Brazen it out!" said Quentin Corn to himself.

"Of course I talk. Whatever *you* think I look like, I am a runaway orphan fellow who's come to this town to do honest work and make my way, and if you need your room, of course I'll—"

"A talking pig," said Pete, sitting on the bed and studying Q thoughtfully. "A walking talking fortune. I *must* be dreaming."

"—of course I'll seek other lodgings—"

"Shut up." Pete bit his lip and went on staring at Q. "Now. Let's get this straight. You're a pig, but you can talk—"

"I talk, but I am not a—"

"I said shut up! You are a pig that's somehow learned to talk. And to fool everybody you're a nice deserving lad making his way. You got them *all* fooled? The whole *town*? I always said this was a backward burg." He waited a moment, then went on muttering to himself. "A pig. You talk. I'm awake." He pinched himself on the leg, hard. "Yup. Wide awake So, the next thing is—how do we turn this into mazoola?"

Q could see that mazoola, like bits and bucks, was money. But how did this lout expect to make money out of somebody who was earning three bucks a week?

Maybe I could rush him, thought Q. He's pretty muscular, but so am I. Maybe I should—

"Okay, it's like this," said Pete. "I'll keep mum about who you are—make that *what* you are—and I'll even let you stay here. I'll move in with you. That'll be nice and cozy. Me and a pig. Well, I've slept with worse. On the road, you can't be fussy. Yeah. Bunkies, that's what we'll be. Give Ma a real boot. She thinks you're the cat's whiskers. Should say the pig's bristles, ha-ha. And while I work this out, how we're gonna do it, I'm keeping my eye on you, brother. Don't you think I'm not."

"How we're going to do what?" Q demanded. "I don't know what you're talking about. I am a boy, a young *man!*"

"Not a stupid dirty pig?"

Q jumped up angrily. "Pigs are not stupid *or* dirty!"

Pete Benway grinned. "See? So stow the act and face it that you and me are gonna make my fortune." He rubbed his chin. "Siddown, siddown. Or I'll poke you in the snoot. Snout."

"You and who else? Can you carry a hundred-pound sack of cement in one hand?"

"Nothing to it. Wanna have a round? Probably break some of Ma's furniture, and break her heart some more. She gets the old heart broken easy."

"Only by one person, I think," said Q, sitting down again. He was going to have to humor this ruffian until he could figure a way to outwit him. I am in the presence, he said to himself with lofty rage, of someone wicked. Emily said she's never met anyone wicked, but she knows this Pete, so she has, only doesn't know it.

Wicked, wicked—

"Carnys," Pete was saying. "That's our ticket. Carnivals. First in small places, till we get our bearings, and then for the Big Town, the Big Top! Boy, oh boy, oh boy! You'll outdraw Jumbo! So—here's how it is. In a few days we'll hit the road, ride the rails out west somewhere, and start there and work our way back. After we get some moola for our first shows, we'll outfit you in funny duds and—boy, oh boy, oh boy—you'll knock 'em dead! You, old hog, are going to make Pete Benway rich, and when I get back to *this* town *next* time, are they ever gonna sit up and take notice!"

Rain slashed against the windows, thunder drummed in the hills. Captive and captor looked at each other with hard suspicious eyes.

"Now, I'm getting out of these rags and then going down and tell my old lady that you and me've met and got along dandy, see?" He reached up to the lintel, where Q had never thought to look, and took down a key. "Meanwhile, chum, I'm gonna lock you in so's you don't get any ideas. You're not gonna spoil *my* chance at the big-time."

Q was silent as the door closed, as the key was turned in the lock. For a long time he sat thinking. Then, in a calm and deliberate way, he made his preparations.

CHAPTER THIRTEEN

aving discovered that the new boarder was a pig, gifted in a marvelous and money-making way with a human tongue, Pete Benway still only attributed to Q a pig's capacity for doing things. In locking the door, he was confident that he had a prisoner. There was, of course, a window in the room, *his* room, and the window overlooked the front porch, and there was a trellis at the side of the porch, but none of this occurred to Pete as a possible means of escape for a pig. Once you locked an animal in someplace, in there he stayed locked.

So he went down to the kitchen whistling, to tell his mother that the new fellow was a peach and they'd just bunk along together. And he made some casual promises about settling down and getting a job, and that made his mother happy.

"Isn't Quentin coming down?" Mrs. Benway asked.

"Quentin? Oh, yeah. Sure, Quentin. Naw, he said he was sleepy. Gonna take a little snoozeroo. How about a game of Parcheesi, Ma?" Parcheesi always got her. That or dominoes. Simple type, his Ma.

Mrs. Benway, overcome, over*joyed* at the sight of Pete's new leaf, forgot about her boarder as she settled down to Parcheesi with her son.

Upstairs, Q was frowning over a piece of paper on which he had managed to crayon a red heart. He'd seen pictures of those in the books Emily had read to him. He wished he'd had time to learn the alphabet, so that he could write kind Mrs. Benway a note. But a crayoned heart, he hoped, would show that he meant he'd been happy with her and enjoyed her food and her company and her pretty house and his chance at the choir and—

Would it tell her all that? Any of that? He wished it would also, *some*how, tell her to give Emily his love and thank her for liking him and reading to him and being his friend.

He sighed, sure that the message was too long and complicated for even a well-drawn heart to get across. His was not especially well drawn. Selecting another crayon, a purple one, he drew, for the second time (and the last time) a careful Q in the center of the heart. His own letter. Q. It looked nice there, right in the middle of the red heart.

He didn't have a pincushion. There was one in Mrs. Benway's bedroom, on her dresser, but no way to get to it. So he folded the paper and put it in his bandanna, along with the money that Mr. Wheatley had given him yesterday, not taking off for the free morning's work at Constable Mears's cottage. And that was only yesterday! He owed Mrs. Benway for board and room, and did not feel he'd done his chores as well as he might have. He tied the neck-scarf carefully and tucked it into his pants pocket.

Then he opened the window, climbed out in the still-pelting rain, turned and closed the window behind him, trotted gingerly down the porch roof, let himself down by the trellis, and dropped to the ground. A rush of water from the drainpipe splashed him as he ran around to the summer kitchen. Opening the door very carefully, he threw the bandanna across the room, saw it land on the floor near Mrs. Benway's rocker, nodded, and took off.

Though it was still afternoon, the day was dark, and Dr. Anthony, going by in his Model T, had the side curtains up against the rain. With his eyes fixed on the road ahead, he did not see Q rush after him and leap to the rear bumper and wrap his arms around the wheelcase. He felt a slight thump. Thumps on this road were always being felt, and Dr. Anthony, on his way to a case well out in the country, paid no heed.

With the wind and the rain in his face, his arms growing weary from their hold on the wheelcase, Q was bounced and bucked along for miles. The sun was beginning to peer out of the black sky like a drowned face when Dr. Anthony turned his car from the dirt road onto a rocky winding uphill lane. Q, unable to hang on any longer, released his hold and tumbled into the trees.

He lay there for a while, not bothering to think. The rain ceased, though all the leaves in the woods continued to drip and shiver. Suddenly the sun sent bright steaming shafts of gold down through the pointed firs, the maples and oaks and birch trees. The scent of the forest floor, of

moss and pine needles and long-fallen leaves drenched by the storm, exhaled a sharp sweetness as the sun's warmth reached down through the branches. The fragrance reached Quentin Corn, lying on a bed of moss, gazing upwards, not thinking.

"What are you doing there?" said a voice nearby. Not a human voice. Animal.

Q turned his head. "Nothing. Lolling."

"I can't understand you. What are you saying?" The owner of the voice emerged from the trees. Q knew at once that he was seeing a wild pig. He'd heard about them from Mr. Quigley and his friends and sons. Those men, with *guns*, hunted wild pigs. How could anyone go with a gun after such a dear little creature as this? Beautiful big head, white tusks, slender flanks. Dainty, dainty as she could be. A little wild pig, and in Q's eyes, wildly pretty.

Seeing her, all his old longing for his old life as a pig (just not as a barrow and barbecue) flooded back. At the same time, just as acutely, he felt the tug of the past seven days. Emily and her merry, kind ways, and the fairy tales at the end of the bean and corn rows. Mrs. Benway's motherly ways, her chicken salad. The choir robes and the singing! Even Mr. Wheatley's gravelly voice. All that called to him.

Between two worlds, he looked at the enchanting stranger and sighed.

"And just what, may I ask, do *you* call yourself?" she said with a superior sniff.

"Oh—a young man, as you can see." But he said it in *pig*. A girl like this, living apart from human beings, wouldn't know their language, the way farm animals did.

Every animal at Quigley's had known just what the people were saying. Except the chickens, who didn't know anything.

"Don't be silly," she was saying. "You're much too good-looking to be a man, even a young one."

"I am?" said Q, pleased. No one back in town had ever called him good-looking. Emily had said he was beautiful—*for a pig*. He did not think that came out to the same kind of compliment as the one he'd just had.

"And what *are* you doing in that outfit?" she went on.

"Wearing it, of course. These are my clothes. Sort of." He got to his feet.

"Well, you look silly. Why are you standing on two legs that way?"

"All men stand on two legs. It's their way."

"It is not your way. Man, indeed. You're a fine big boar and you should get out of those—those *things*—and get your feet on the ground. All four of them."

"And what then?" he asked. "Go back to Quigley's to be barrowed and barbecued?"

She looked horror-struck. "Was that what was going to happen to you?"

"It was. So I ran away and became a young fellow with his way to make in a little town where everybody thought I *was* a young fellow. Just about everybody. I ran away from there because a fellow was going to try to make *his* fortune, turning *me* into a carnival freak."

"You don't have to go back to Quigley's to be cooked, *or* to some town where you have to pretend to be something you aren't. And you don't have to keep running away, either." Q waited, knowing she would tell him what he should do, and she did. "You can join our band," she said. "We don't belong to any farmer and we have nothing to do with town life. We are free pigs in the wild."

"Free pigs," Q mused. "There's really such a thing?"

"You bet your acorns."

"Farmers go after you with guns. I know that much."

"I'm not saying we're free of fear, or free of peril, but when they come at us with guns, we can run. We've got a chance. What can a pig in a pen do, when the farmer comes after him?"

Q shuddered.

"As for living in *town*, pretending to be a man! That's just silly. How long could you get away with that?"

"Not much longer, I guess," Q admitted.

"Well?"

He tore off his clothes, dropped to his four sturdy feet.

Then a strange thing happened. He forgot that he had ever been anything but a big brown boar. His seven days of young manhood fell to the forest floor with the pants, the shirt, the painter's cap. Leaving the little bundle of rags to rot away with fallen leaves and pine needles, he went off with the beautiful stranger to begin the life he was meant for.

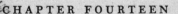

CHAPTER FOURTEEN

And what of the people in the town he'd left behind him? How did they take his sudden departure? Very calmly, since most of them had been unaware of his arrival.

Mrs. Benway missed him most of all. She found his little farewell packet in the summer kitchen and was surprised at the pang it brought.

After all, she thought, he was only here a week. I can't have got that fond of him. But she put the corner of her apron to her eyes to wipe away a few tears that *would* fall.

Pete, coming in to demand food, said irritably, "Now what?"

Mrs. Benway shoved the neck-scarf with its contents into her pocket. "Quentin's gone for good. You drove him away, of course. For all your talk of liking him."

Pete, enraged at being cheated out of his fortune, yelled, "What d'ya mean, *liking* him? He was a PIG!"

"He was a lot neater than you ever were."

"I'm not talking about neatness! I'm saying he was a real pig. Not a *person*—a pig, a pig, a pig!"

"That will be enough of that. Isn't it enough that you forced a fine young lad out of a town where he was making a place for himself, and working hard, and making friends, and going to be in the *choir* . . . isn't it enough that you've sent him out on the road again after only a few days, without saying nasty things about him? You won. He's gone. But don't you talk about him that way, because I won't have it, do you hear?"

Pete stamped around the room in a fury. "You don't seem to be getting it through your head! Are you plain dumb, or what?"

"You stop talking to your mother that way, young man," said Mr. Wheatley, looming at the screen door. "If I hear that tone again, I'll beat the tar out of you."

Pete spun around. "Who d'ya think *you* are, you old fool, telling me how I'm supposed to talk to my own mother?"

"Ada," said Mr. Wheatley. "Do I have your permission to give this boy some straight talk?"

Mrs. Benway looked from her son to her long-time suitor. "Oh, I don't care," she said. "Henry, Quentin has gone."

"Gone where?"

"Who knows. He left me a little note. Which is *quite* private," she added. She was not going to let anyone know that apparently poor Quentin, poor orphan, had never learned to read or write. That poor little Q, so carefully crayoned. That shakily outlined heart . . . enough to make a body cry. "A note," she continued, "and the whole three dollars you'd paid him, Henry. For his board and room." Again the apron at the eye.

"Holy cow!" Pete howled. "I mean, holy SWINE! You're crazy, all of you!"

Ignoring him, Mr. Wheatley patted Mrs. Benway's hand. "I guess, after all, Q is shiftless, like the rest of these young fellows. But he's honest. Which is more," he said, glaring at Pete, "than can be said for some."

Pete beat the side of his head with his fists. "This's a nuthouse . . . a booby hatch! You both oughta be strapped down to something!"

"That does it!" growled Mr. Wheatley, starting forward.

"Henry!" Mrs. Benway cried out.

"Get away from me!" yelled Pete.

Mr. Wheatley stopped, looked over his shoulder, and said, "Ada, for the last time, absolutely the last, I ask you to marry me. Now, make up your mind quick, or you'll never see me in this house again."

"Hah!" said Pete.

"Yes," said Mrs. Benway.

"All right," said Mr. Wheatley, turning back to Pete, "this is how it goes. You either shape up or ship out. You work, you talk to your mother respectful, you never say one mean thing again about Quentin Corn, because we happen to like him and we don't like to hear our friends bad-mouthed. Got all that?"

"And if I . . . won't *shape up*?"

"You got a choice and you know what it is. So, what's it to be?"

Pete started out of the room, halted, looked back through narrowed eyes. "I'll think it over," he said, and stamped off.

"And now, Ada," said Mr. Wheatley, with the brightest expression she had ever seen on his face, "let's you and me make plans."

It wasn't long before they'd both forgotten Mrs. Benway's young boarder, and Mrs. Wheatley never got around to showing Emily the farewell message that had tried to say so much with such limited means.

And Emily.

On the day of the Sunday dinner, when Emily had urged Q to stay for dessert and croquet, not sounding as if she cared if he did or did not, the broken vase remained on the floor for hours, and the fate of the shawl was all at once of no importance. Because suddenly, and violently, Emily was sick.

She was put to bed with a temperature. Cold compresses were applied, and mustard plasters. Mr. Scott ran across the green to fetch Dr. Anthony. He, however, did not get back from his long call out in the country until late evening. By then, Emily was delirious, and so she remained for several days, in a dark and fevered world that took no account of family or friends, or daylight or nightfall, no account of herself, her own being.

One morning, nearly a week after Q had gone to begin his second new life, she woke and looked about vaguely, spellbound and uncertain until her gaze rested on her father, sitting in a chair close to her bed.

"Well," he said, smiling and rubbing his eyes with thin fingers. "Emily. Here you are, with us again." He picked up one of her hands, holding it in both of his.

"I've been sick, haven't I, Papa?"

"Yes, dearest. Very sick."

"And I might have *died*?" she said, interested in such a grown-up possibility, now that she had escaped it.

Mr. Emerson did not flinch from facts with his daughters. "Very sick people," he said, "seem to . . . to depart from themselves, from the people who love them. They make their way back very slowly. Some . . . just journey on and never do return. But here you are," he said again. "Back with us. And now, right this minute, you will start to get better. And I," he said, getting to his feet with a shaky smile, "am going to tell your mother and sisters." He turned in the doorway. "Emily, I have had many happy moments in my life, but I think, I do think, that I am happier now than I have ever been before. Yes, I do believe that," he said, hesitating, as if he could not leave her. "God has been good to us. So good. I must tell them," he said, and hurried off.

Though it was still summer, a breeze came through the open window and Emily pulled the patchwork quilt (one of Sophy's) over her shoulders. Then she lay quietly, cozy, tired, content.

She'd had all kinds of dreams in that flushed and restless world she'd sweated through. Some horrible, too horrible to recall, and so they drifted to the outposts of her mind, to lie perhaps in wait for future years, or perhaps to molder away quite forgotten. Some, she thought, watching her toes wriggle under the quilt, kind of cute and funny. She'd made friends with a pig in one of them. He'd worn clothes and been very very clever and dear and had had his own nice funny name—Quentin Corn. That had been the nicest dream she'd ever had. But she never mentioned it to anyone. Her mother said that people who told their dreams should be forced to listen to everyone else's, so naturally no one in her family ever told.

And the Emersons did not mention Emily's friend, Quentin, thinking perhaps she was too hurt at his running off without coming to say goodbye, or even leaving her a note. They thought his behavior quite bad, after all Emily had tried to do for him. Presently, like Mrs. Benway and Mr. Wheatley, they forgot him.

Then there was Mr. Carberry, the only other person, it might be thought, to be afflicted by Q's departure. But Mr. Carberry didn't have the nature for affliction. He told himself that probably the lad's voice would have broken before the choir's Christmas program, and all the work of training him go for nothing.

There was one more person whose life had been, ever so lightly, touched by Q.

After five years of nearly total reserve, Andy Mears burst into speech, and thereafter the flow of his words was dammed only by sleep, and not always then. Asleep or awake, in all the torrent of his conversation as he grew, Andy remained a boy who could keep a secret.

He grew up to have the finest boy's soprano that the

town had ever known, and Mr. Carberry caught him early. One day, when Andy was ten, he and Mr. Carberry were rehearsing his part in the Easter chorale.

"You know," Mr. Carberry said reflectively, when Andy had hit an especially high sweet note, "you remind me of a boy I'd quite forgotten. You wouldn't remember him, it was so long ago. Quentin, his name was. Quentin something. He had a voice rather like yours. Not, of course, as wonderful. And there was a—I can only call it a kind of musical *squeal* in his upper register. Quite distinctive, it was."

"I do so remember him," said Andy. "He came with Mr. Wheatley, on my birthday, when Mr. Wheatley gave me the little wooden bird-whistle. See, I still have it," he said, taking the whistle from his pocket. "His name was Quentin Corn, and he was really a—" he paused and smiled. "He was really a very nice fellow."

THE END

All this happened a long time ago.